'Tis the Season

AF270761

An Anthology from The East Texas Writers' Association

White Bird Publications
P.O Box 586
Diana, Texas 75640
www.whitebirdpublications.com

This is a work of fiction. Names, characters, places, and incidents either are the product of the author's imagination or are used fictitiously. Any resemblance to actual events, locals or persons, living or dead, is entirely coincidental.

Copyright©2013 East Texas Writer's Association
The Christmas Promise, & Seasons of Change - Elizabeth Baker
Kat and the Cougar, Wanna Take A Swim?, The Cheer of Autumn, & Bless It All Burt - Jeannie Faulkner Barber
The Right Call & The Bassicus Angleris of East Texas - Vivra P. Beene
The Cabin - Evelyn M. Byrne
My Frosty Valentine, By the Sweat of the Brow, Grandma's Cactus Garden - Brinda Carey
Traveling Sands, I Dream of Horses!, Sweet Cherie Pie, O My Heart! - Judith Victoria Douglas
A Princess in Her Own Right, Mother Remembers, On the Mend, &Princess Envy - Kimmie Easley
Summertime - Janice Ernest
Nathaniel and Caroline - Ann Everett
Escape, The Song That Changed Everything, & The Shoe Fit the Wrong Sister - Lynn Hobbs
A Christmas Like No Other, Joshua's Tree, & Yellow Bus - Gay Ingram
The Woman in the Wall Paper - Simon Lang
Tracks & Summer - Jean Lauzier
Making Christmas, Memories of Christmas, The Easter Bunny's Gift, & The Easter Gift - C. R. Myers,
Twirl Mom's Revenge - Kimberli O'Brien
The Christmas Without Presents - Kassy Paris
The Wizard's Coins & Shadowlon - Larence Shaddox

Wanted: New Home - Judy Walker
Cowboy Philosophy - Denny L. Youngblood

Cover art by E. Kusch

Editors: Jeannie Faulkner Barber
         Darlene A. Hartman
         Jean Lauzier
         Cat Myers
         Kassy Paris

All rights reserved. No part of this book may be reproduced or transmitted in any form or by any electronic or mechanical means, including photocopying, recording or by any information storage and retrieval system, without the written permission of the author, except where permitted by law.

LCCN: 2013943193
ISBN: 978-1-937690-41-0

PRINTED IN THE UNITED STATES OF AMERICA.

If you purchased this book without a cover, you should be aware that this book is stolen property. It was reported as "unsold and destroyed" to the publisher and neither the author nor the publisher has received any payment for this "stripped book."

Dedication
By
Gay Ingram

Since I hold the longest-standing membership of East Texas Writers Association, I've been asked to write the dedication for our latest group effort.

With a nod of gratitude toward those who came before, I dedicate this anthology to all those fabulous and dedicated writers who have been, and are presently, a part of ETWA.

It is only as we learn from those who came before that we are enabled to grow in this empowering craft of writing.

Acknowledgements

There are many people who helped make this anthology possible and a sincere thanks goes to each of them, especially **Jeannie Faulkner Barber** and **Kassy Paris** for gathering all the submissions and a first round of edits.

Next, the authors whose work is included. Without them, there would be no anthology. Not only did they submit great stories and poems but worked with our editors to make each the best it could be. Many of the included authors have other works available so be sure to check them out.

A very special thanks goes to our editors. **Kassy Paris, C. R. Myers, Jean Lauzier,** and **Darlene Hartman**. We appreciate your hard work.

Evelyn M. Byrne, thanks for wrestling with the formatting and all the details involved.

Thank you White Bird Publications, for a great cover and final book.

Lastly, we give thanks for each of you, the reader. You are the reason we write.

Table of Contents:

Biographies

The East Texas Writer's Association began as The Longview Writer's Association in 1976. By 1981, the group had grown to include members from areas as far as Texarkana, Lufkin, Shreveport and Dallas so a new, more appropriate name was needed. ETWA's membership represents a mixture of writers, published and not, writing in all genres.

We thank all the past and present officers of The East Texas Writers' Association for their hard work and dedication in keeping this club a viable part of the East Texas writing community.

Present ETWA Officers

President: *Jean Lauzier*
Vice-President: *Larence Shaddox*
Secretary: *Kimmie Easley*
Treasurer: *Evelyn M. Byrne*
Publicist: *Kenisha Odoms*
Roughdraft Editor: *Kassy Paris*
Special Projects Chair: *Jeannie Barber*
Web Master: *Evelyn M. Byrne*

'Tis the Season

White Bird
Publications

Winter

Tracks
By
Jean Lauzier

Leiannah stood at the edge of the forest staring at the tracks in the snow. Tracks bigger than any she'd seen. She knelt, placed a gloved hand in the print, her fingers almost touching the edges. A breeze teased her hair, chilled her face. A twig snapped somewhere nearby. Chills ran up her spine as she imagined it studying her. She'd caught glimpses of it several times over the past weeks, but it always managed to eat the meat she'd left for it without being seen.

Another shiver ran up her spine. Leiannah stood, pulled her coat tighter. She glanced at the cabin in the clearing behind her. Smoke rose from the chimney. She should go back, back to warmth and safety. Taking a deep breath, she followed the tracks into the forest.

Snow crunched with each step. She ducked under branches weighed down with their covering of snow. Her breath left vapor trails in the air. The wind shifted the snow under the trees, covering the tracks in places. In others, it swept across the ground leaving bare patches of frozen earth.

Leiannah halted at a fork in the path and stared at the tracks. It had circled, gone this way and that, taken both paths and returned, even gone off into the forest. She gazed around, not sure where she was, and listened to the forest. Left, she'd go left. It was the least traveled but felt right. Leiannah pulled her scarf tighter, let out a breath, and strode onward.

She held onto branches and shrubs, her boots slipping as the path sloped downward. A twig snapped to her right, she jerked, spun around. Her boot stepped on a snow-covered rock and slipped. She grabbed for a limb, missed, and fell. Snow softened her fall but helped her slide down the hill. A pine tree stopped her descent when she rolled into it. She climbed to her feet, eyes focused on top of the hill. She had to get back up there. One step, then two.

Grabbing a small shrub, she pulled herself up another step. Her foot slipped. The shrub shifted, gave way, and Leiannah tumbled down the hill again. She rolled and slid, the trees a blur until she came to rest in a clearing. Sitting up, she looked around. This wasn't a clearing. Ice cracked not far from where she sat. The river. Must get off the ice. She struggled to her feet, slipping, sliding on the ice. Another crack, this time much closer. She'd managed to stand, took a step. The ice shattered, plunging her into the water. She clawed at the ice, tried to scream but got a mouthful of icy water instead. Water filled her boots, pulled her down.

A soft warmth surrounded her. She opened her eyes, tried to sit up.

Rest easy, child. You are safe now. Sleep, restore yourself.

Leiannah gazed into amber eyes, sighed, and drifted to sleep.

A Christmas Like No Other
By
Gay Ingram

That Christmas day dawned much like all the other days had since my arrival, a balmy day whose temperatures were tempered by a salt-laden breeze. The year was 1959 and I was in Honolulu, Hawaii, my Coast Guard husband's most recent duty station. Because he had transferred here from Texas before our son was born, this would be our first Christmas to celebrate together as a family. Our off-base living accommodation was a minuscule walk-up studio, one of four on the second floor of a plain wooden apartment building. The only outdoor space available was a concrete-bound patch of green imitating a lawn and dominated by a sprawling mango tree. Bright sunshine and warm temperatures denied the reality that this day was December twenty-fifth.

Inside our tiny apartment, we had no room for a tree, not even a tabletop one. Piled on and spilling over one of the two upholstered chairs that defined our living room area were presents delivered by the U. S. Mail from family in Texas and Connecticut. Looking back, my mind's eye saw the mad scramble of kids rushing down the staircase to the tree in the living room. Eager anticipation shone on all faces as we perched on edges of seats waiting for our names to be called and handed a present. It seemed the walls of our home bulged with barely contained joy. Each time those packages caught my eye, an intense sense of isolation and raw awareness of the thousands of miles that separated me from my family would grip me.

But though the setting didn't resemble familiar

Christmases of our past—family gatherings for holiday meals, special services at church to commemorate the season, gay parties with friends—the reason for the season filled our hearts even here in Honolulu and we determined to make the best of the circumstances.

Not even waiting to dress, we eagerly read names on presents, distributed them to one another and soon each had a small stack waiting to be opened. Delaying my curiosity, I watched as my toddler fumbled with the first gift, an odd-shaped package wrapped in flowery red and white paper. Even before all the wrapping was removed, David stared in fascination at a gray plastic dump truck. We watched with pleasure as he raised and lowered the bed of the truck and wheeled the toy about the littered floor.

Upon opening a gift from my family, my husband broke into laughter. They had sent him a special game. The box said "Texas Checkers." To emphasize that everything is bigger in Texas, each playing piece filled his palm.

In no time, crumpled paper and discarded ribbon covered the remaining floor space. We perched on the unmade bed, showing each other our new treasures and laughed at our son's efforts to discover the mysteries of a large brown piggy bank. Then we hurried through breakfast and dressed as my husband had invited a shipmate, another transplant from Texas, to spend the day with us.

Our guest arrived and soon the men were sitting cross-legged on the floor, their attention focused on the plastic playing board of a checker game between them. While my son napped in the playpen/bed, I hurried to prepare our Christmas dinner. No turkey, nor pumpkin or pecan pies that year. I didn't have space to prepare anything so elaborate. My kitchen area in that apartment was so compact I could stand in one spot and reach the table, stove, sink, and refrigerator.

We squeezed a borrowed chair up to a table with barely space to spread three place settings shoved against the wall. An old-fashioned, wooden high chair contained our well-rested son as we enjoyed our simple meal.

With stomachs full, we decided an excursion would be an ideal way to spend this lovely day. So we piled into the well-used '42 Plymouth my husband had acquired second-hand for transportation to his ship and back. Our destination was the observation overlook at National Memorial Cemetery of the Pacific. This monument to our fallen heroes is located in Punchbowl Crater, the site of a long-blown-out volcano and just minutes away from downtown Honolulu.

As a sea breeze ruffled my hair and our son wriggled within the tight embrace of his father's arms, we looked down at the rows and rows of white crosses seeming to march into eternity. The sight filled me with a heaviness of soul; tears trickled unbidden down my cheeks as I considered the patriots, the many young men who had given their lives to right a wrong in this world.

My thoughts moved to the One whose birthday we celebrated this day. He also willingly gave His life to make it possible for mankind to once again have a right relationship with His Heavenly Father.

The next year would find our family back stateside, my husband out of the service and our family able to celebrate Christmas with extended family once again. It would be a traditional Christmas; our tree would glitter with decorations and trimmings; signs of festivity would be hung throughout the house. We would attend Christmas Eve service in our church to see the familiar story re-enacted, smile at the childish voices quavering with nervousness, feel the blessing of being surrounded by those we loved. Christmas day would be spent at Grandmother's house, surrounded by family eager to share the latest happenings while excited children showed off the new toys.

There have been many Christmases since that first one our family celebrated in an unfamiliar place. I know now that it isn't the exterior trimmings that make the season festive and joyous. It is the sure knowledge that love is able to conquer all difficult circumstances.

The Christmas Promise
By
Elizabeth Baker

When the bell rang indicating the elevator was stopping on the seventh floor, Jennifer pushed her way past the fat man with a briefcase. "Excuse me," she said politely. "I'm going down." She could never understand why people stood in front of elevators that weren't going their direction, but then, there were a lot of mysteries in life.

"Hey, Jennifer! Merry Christmas!" a woman's voice called from the back on the crowded cab.

"Brenda! Merry Christmas, yourself!" She threaded her way through the press of strangers until she was standing shoulder to shoulder with her friend. "Got any plans for tomorrow?"

"Only what you would expect." She sighed. It had been a long day at the office and everyone was ready for the holiday to begin. "I still have to bake another batch of cookies. The kids will be up before dawn to find what Santa brought and Brad's parents are coming over for Christmas dinner." Brenda yawned behind her hand. "I sure am glad Christmas only comes once a year or I'd never make it."

"Sounds like you have a lot left to do. I can understand a single gal like me working on Christmas Eve, but you have a family. I don't know how you do it."

"Yeah, well, I've got to pay for all those Christmas goodies, you know."

They rode in silence for a moment then Brenda smiled mischievously. "Speaking of marital status, I don't suppose you're expecting a special Christmas gift from Caleb? Like maybe an engagement ring?"

"Maybe." Jennifer's cheeks burned. "Who knows what might happen with Christmas magic in the air? His flight from Chicago is due in at eleven tonight and he promised he would be at my apartment for dinner at one. He said he had something special to show me."

The elevator stopped and sliding doors opened into the polished marble lobby of Blackmore Consulting Company. "Well, that sounds like a June wedding to me!" Brenda teased as they headed for the exit.

A surprising number of people were milling about and Jennifer thought the place looked more like a mall than an office building on Christmas Eve. "The big city rat race never stops," she said as the friends parted just outside the revolving door.

The sky was already dusky and Christmas lights twinkled from every window while smiling people rushed past decorated lampposts. She sighed. Maybe the rat race couldn't be avoided, but looking at a city street dressed for the holidays made you remember that it wasn't all bad. There was another side to New York. A joyous side that nothing else could match.

Back at her apartment, Jennifer began preparation for the Christmas feast. She would serve a low-fat version of her grandmother's stuffing and the Cornish hens she picked up at the deli should be just right for two. Soon the aroma of cornbread filled her small space and cranberry salad cooled in the fridge. Christmas really was a magical time.

By six-thirty, she was dressed in a comfortable cotton robe, sipping cappuccino and thinking of life back home. Mississippi had been a great place to grow up, but after her parents died, there just didn't seem to be any reason to stay. Neither of her sisters could understand why she was attracted to the city, but then, they had never understood many things about the baby of the family. Most years,

Jennifer yielded to their pleading and flew back home for Christmas. But, not this year. Since Caleb came into her life, everything she wanted was right here.

Caleb. Thoughts of the tall, shy young man settled peacefully on her heart. They had known each other for only four months, yet she could hardly remember life without him. Caleb was steady and wonderfully predictable. She often knew what he was thinking before he said it, and he seemed to be able to do the same with her thoughts. They laughed and shared deep, silent moments. They enjoyed the same sports, were members of the same church, and even had similar political ideals.

An hour drifted slowly by. Usually Jennifer would have been agitated over some TV-news report, or on the phone chatting with her sisters, but not tonight. Instead, she turned on a CD of familiar carols, darkened the room and watched the snow fall on a city of colored lights. God had sent the promised Savior and Caleb had promised to come for Christmas dinner. Both concepts brought peaceful assurance to her soul.

It was still snowing when Jennifer woke the next morning, but not bad enough to cause concern; just a light frosting to make this Christmas a white one. She stretched luxuriously then threw back the covers. Cool air washed over her warm limbs giving an exhilarating start to the day. She rushed through dressing and headed for the kitchen with a light step.

A CD played sweet melodies of *Silent Night* and *Away in a Manger* while she set the table for two. She fairly danced around the kitchen while slicing potatoes as *Jingle Bells* filled the air and by eleven-thirty she was nervously watching the door, hoping Caleb might decide to come a little early.

By the time the clock struck one, Jennifer could scarcely contain herself. He had promised he would come for Christmas and Caleb was never late. She paced. She turned off the CD and watched the TV weather channel.

No problem with the snow. All streets clear in the big city.

It was shortly after one-thirty when she called the airport. All flights were on time. The recorded voice gave a politically correct response to the season. "Have a Happy Holiday."

At two she called his apartment. No answer. She tried his cell. It was either dead or her number was blocked.

At two-fifteen she began to cry. He had promised.

The rest of the afternoon was a blur. She wanted to call her sisters, but they would be celebrating with their families. No need to ruin everyone's holiday just because her boyfriend jilted her. Besides, Christie would just tell her how happy she ought to be that Caleb's unfaithfulness showed now rather than after a wedding, and Ginny would only cry and beg her to come home.

The afternoon faded and for a second evening Jennifer stood at her window watching the Christmas lights in the street below. Tears came intermittently now but in her soul she knew she would be crying for a long, long time to come. He had promised.

She didn't know why she turned back on the CD player. Maybe she just couldn't stand the silence any longer. But, the carols were strangely comforting. "It came upon the midnight clear, that glorious song of old." The familiarity of the words was like a warm blanket on a cold night. Then the choir began the third verse and the song took on new meaning. "...*beneath life's crushing load...form...bending low...Who toil...painful steps and slow...glad...golden hours...swiftly on the wing...hear the angels sing.*" Maybe Caleb was not the type to keep promises, but the God of all creation surely kept his. She could hope in that.

She was jolted from spiritual considerations by a loud, insistent doorbell.

"Yes?"

"It's me, Caleb. Can I come up?"

Silence.

"Jennifer, I can explain. Please?"

Not trusting her voice, she didn't answer; only pushed the buzzer releasing the door at street level. A few moments later, she heard his knock.

During the two-minute interval between hearing his voice and his knock, she had gone through every emotion from elation to anger to fear. She breathed deeply and waited for this second knock before turning the knob with her still shaking hand.

"Am I welcome?" Caleb asked timidly.

"I don't know. Should you be?" She backed up to let him in, turning away her face so she wouldn't have to look at him.

"I tried to keep my promise. Really I did. It was the snow."

"Oh, stop it Caleb. I checked the airlines. All flights are coming and going on time."

"The snow yesterday. In Buffalo. My flight was rerouted from Chicago."

"So, all the telephones were out, too?"

"I didn't call because I didn't want to worry you and thought if I could get a flight today, I would still be on time."

For the first time she looked directly in his eyes. "And exactly when did you find out that was not going to happen?"

"About one when my rescheduled flight from Buffalo landed 'on time'."

"It's now six in the evening."

"Flat tire at the airport."

"You never heard of cell phones?"

He fished in the pocket of his over coat and pulled out his phone holding it up for her inspection. "Dead battery."

Jennifer was silent but at least her hands had stopped shaking.

"Honey, I'm sorry," He looked at her with pleading, blue eyes and after a moment moved toward her. "I really am." When she didn't resist, he slowly took her in his arms.

It took another three hours for the tension to totally resolve between them, but after a cold, late dinner, they were able to snuggle on the sofa listening to carols and watching the snow.

"Jennifer," he breathed into her hair. "Remember I said I had something special to show you this Christmas?"

She tensed. "Yes."

He pulled a small box from his pocket and opened the lid. The diamonds were small but glistened brightly in the candlelight. "I am only a man. If you'll have me for a husband, there might be many times I fail to keep my promises to you. But, I tell you now, in the name of the One who always keeps His, I'll always try."

Making Christmas
A True Story
By
C. R. Myers

Christmas always started early at our house. The holiday was too big to squeeze into just one day—or one week—or even one month. One year we began especially early. Our only child was eight, so when she suggested we start the festivities a full month before we'd ever done before, her vote carried a heavy weight. The date was October first.

I reminded her of the two holidays ahead of us, the two we would be preempting to begin our Christmas traditions. She nodded, her expression serious. "There wouldn't be less Halloween or Thanksgiving," she explained with an attitude of patience, "just more Christmas." It was my turn to nod. How could anyone object to having more Christmas?

We began listening to Christmas music, and I unpacked our favorite holiday videos. Outside, autumn leaves fell from the trees, and carved pumpkins grinned in neighborhood windows. Inside, we cut strips of red and green construction paper and listened to the rich vocals of Bing Crosby.

Halloween came and went, while *The Grinch Stole Christmas* and *"Chestnuts Roasted by an Open Fire."* Thanksgiving grew near as did our annual Christmas project. Some years we made ornaments. Some years we made gifts. My daughter liked to say we "made" Christmas. This year the project would be more involved than most.

For years we collected cookie cutters of various shapes and sizes and kept them together in a special red velvet bag. When my daughter was young, the cookie cutters shaped play dough and mud cakes. A few years and a few spins in the dishwasher later, they shaped sugar cookies. Stars, bells, angels, reindeer, rabbits, and kittens were among our favorites as well as about a dozen different Santas.

This year the cookie cutters would shape ornaments. I reached for the largest bowl I owned, and my daughter retrieved her step stool. We read the recipe. Flour, salt, and water. Sounded easy enough. We took turns stirring the ingredients inside the huge, wooden bowl, but the fun came with the kneading. By the time it was done, we were floured from head to toe.

Cutting the shapes was fun as well, but our greatest pleasure was the painting. Blue and yellow bells, pink angels with blonde hair, gingerbread men in coveralls, hearts and elves, and red suited Santas. We let our imaginations run wild, until the counter top was filled with brightly colored ornaments.

Strung with red satin ribbon, the ornaments made the Christmas tree beautiful. We made ornament sets for the grandparents and a few extra ornaments as gifts. For years afterward every Christmas included samples of our dough ornaments. We took them gingerly from their tissue paper wrapping and handled them with care as if they were valuable and precious.

I'd get a catch in my throat, seeing them hanging on the tree season after season. They looked as beautiful as the first night we hung them. But dough is a fragile medium and not meant to last forever. One by one the ornaments slowly disappeared—gone, but never to be forgotten.

We learned something that year, in our almost three-month season of Christmas. Christmas is more than a date on a calendar. Christmas is its own season and its own time. Christmas starts when we start it, and it ends when we end it. Christmas doesn't make Christmas. We do. Such a simple idea, but one often overlooked. Christmas is what we make it.

INGREDIENTS

8 cups all-purpose flour
2 cups salt
3 cups water

DIRECTIONS

Preheat oven to 300 degrees F (150 degrees C).
Combine the flour, salt, and water; mix well and knead for 10 minutes. Roll out on a lightly floured surface.
Cut into desired shapes and make holes for hanging. Bake for 30 minutes; allow to cool.
Decorate with poster paints or tube paints. Allow to dry and spray with clear polyurethane on both sides to preserve. Use ribbon or yarn pieces to hang.

My Frosty Valentine
By
Brinda Carey

Hoping Chad's basketball practice wasn't running late, Amy stood by his car in the parking lot of the high school. She tugged his letter jacket tightly across her chest and breathed deeply of his lingering scent, imagining her face pressed against his chest. Her steamy breath did little to warm her fingers, so with one hand gripping the collar to her face, she slid the other deep into his pocket where her fingers closed. They closed upon a card. The embossed hearts across the envelope made her smile. He remembered. She pulled out the Valentine for a quick glimpse before he arrived and froze after reading the first line: "To my darling Sarah."

The Wizard's Coins
By
Larence Shaddox

Robert led his horse deeper into the woods with reins in one hand and sword in the other. He stopped in a clearing. The sparse moonlight peeked from behind the clouds for a few moments, making the snow glow.

"Well, Falstaff," he whispered. "I think we are far enough away from the road to be safe from any highwaymen." He removed the saddle as he spoke. "This clearing even has some grass poking up through the snow for you. It will go nicely with what little grain I have."

Falstaff flicked his ears. Robert took the last handful of grain from the pouch fastened to the back of his saddle, and fed them to Falstaff. Robert deposited his gear beside an immense tree on the edge of the clearing and examined the behemoth of a tree. The trunk looked to measure six or seven feet in diameter.

Falstaff snorted at the grain shortage and moved to eating the grass.

Robert collected pine-straw and covered the ground just outside the clearing which felt more secure. Then he placed the horse blanket on top of the ground cover for his bed.

He stood, touched the tree, and whispered. "Oh, Mighty Oak, king of the forest, I ask your forgiveness at my disturbing your home. Please watch over me tonight and protect my back." He laid his bow, quiver, and dagger beside his bed. With his back to the tree, he pulled the last piece of jerky from his tunic pocket and chewed the dry strip of meat.

After he consumed his sparse supper, he lay down, covering himself and the weapons. His dark brown hair blended with the camouflage offered by the cover. His appearance was more like a hump of dirt in the woods. Only his tanned face was exposed.

The wind blew and snow drifted down from the tree limbs, landing on the blanket blending it with the rest of the area, so that after a while, he could not have been seen. Robert wiggled a few times to get comfortable, and closed his eyes.

Falstaff snorted once in the dark from across the clearing and stepped into the edge of the woods as he was trained and blended into the vegetation.

Robert relaxed into the darkness of slumber.

An unknown time later, something brought him from his deep sleep. The edge of the quilt moved ever so slightly as he grasped his dagger. He didn't know what was to come but he would be prepared. His eyes popped open then squinted against a bright light emanated from the center of the clearing.

The light faded and a man stood in its place. He wore long, gray robes and carried a staff. A pale light emitted from the end of it. His hair hung to his waist in back and his beard halfway down his chest. Topping his head was a broad, floppy hat. Its brim cast a shadow upon his face. A long, slim sword hung from his belt. He looked about the clearing, stepped over to the tree, and laid his right hand upon it.

"Leatadow, moindela due passeque."

Suddenly, the side of the tree opened like a door, missing Robert's head by a fraction as it exposed the hollowed interior. The stranger stepped inside the tree.

"Ah, you guard well these evils, Leatadow." He stepped out and laid a hand upon the tree again.

"Leatadow, moindela due holtem." The magical door closed on the tree. The wizard returned to the center of the clearing and vanished in a bright light.

Robert lay in the ensuing darkness, staring toward the empty clearing. An hour later, the morning light found him still wide-eyed and unmoving, waiting for the return of the wizard.

A gray fox trotted into to the clearing. Its ears perked up, and it looked in the direction of the young man as it sniffed the air, then dashed away into the woods.

Robert stood and sheathed his dagger.

"Falstaff, you okay?"

The horse trotted to his master. Robert rubbed Falstaff's head as he examined the tree, knowing somewhere in it was a door. Yet he found no signs of a crack. No hinges. No mechanism.

"What were his words, Falstaff?" He stood with his hands on his hips. "Leatadow, moindela due holtem?"

Nothing happened. He scratched his head. "No, that was when he left. Leatadow, moindela due passeque."

Still nothing happened.

He rubbed his neck and scrunched up his face as he scrutinized the tree. He leaned with his hand against the tree. "I know I pronounced it the same. Leatadow, moindela due passeque."

The tree pushed against his hand and Robert jumped back. The magical portal opened. He gazed into the hollow tree. "So, I have to touch it." He placed his hand on the tree and spoke, "Leatadow, moindela due holtem."

The door closed and disappeared.

"Leatadow, moindela due passeque." The door opened. "Hey look, Falstaff, I can do magic."

The horse merely flicked his ears.

"I've heard that wizards leave traps on things like this." He picked up a handful of grass and tossed it inside as he jumped back, expecting a lightning bolt to strike him.

Nothing happened.

He drew his dagger and poked the interior quickly before jumping back.

Again, nothing happened.

He boldly stepped into the opening. "No traps." He laughed. "Not a very wise wizard."

The tree was hollowed out for about a four-foot circle to almost six feet in height. Narrow shelves lined its walls. The shelves contained scrolls, bottles of all sizes and colors, cloth or parchment wrapped bundles, and boxes made of wood. Just at his eye level was a small metal chest. He eased the lid open. His eyes grew wide.

He gazed upon gold coins. Some of them showed traces of dried blood. He grasped a handful and stepped out of the tree into the light.

"Robert Wayne Thomas, you have found a wizard's stash. He hides his coins, potions, scrolls, and no telling what else in there. There must be a hundred crowns in that chest."

A hawk flew into the clearing and settled on a limb. It sat and watched as he fingered the coins. Robert looked about, suddenly afraid of robbers. He pressed his hand against the tree and spoke the words to close the door then sat back against the tree in contemplation.

It would have been obvious to any onlooker his conscious was arguing with him.

He stacked the coins up in his hand as he spoke aloud, "I have never stolen anything in my life, Falstaff. I have never so much as taken a crumb of bread that I had not rightfully earned or not been given to me. Lord knows there have been times that I could have and needed to." He counted a dozen coins in his hand.

"It wasn't easy growing up an orphan and trying to earn a living on my own. I climbed and choked in chimneys, cleaning them out until I grew too big to fit in them. I carried twice my weight loading wagons until I couldn't take another step. I've shoveled muck out of barn stalls. I've plowed and fertilized fields." He dropped the coins one at a time into his other hand.

Clink. Clink. Clink.

"Everything I own is properly paid for by my own blood and sweat. Even you. I worked all last year for scarcely more than food and a blanket while I lived in Master Hansen's drafty barn so as to pay for you."

The coins jingled.

"Why did he go accuse me of stealing from him? I have no need for his old box. Aye, twas a pretty box and had real gems embedded in the lid and them fancy foreign words written on it and all. 'I've no need for frippery of that sort."

Falstaff stood looking at Robert.

"There's enough coin in there to buy me a farm, Falstaff and nice size one, at that. I could grow my own food and support a family." He spoke as he stacked the coins on the ground between his legs. He counted them a time or two more as he argued with himself.

"I could have carrots for you to eat. I'd grow wheat and corn for breads, beets, onions, potatoes. 'I'd have chickens to lay eggs, big ones, one to a breakfast.". There would be a cow for milk to go with the peach cobbler my wife would make. Why, I could plant an orchard plumb full of fruit trees for making all sorts of pies and jams to spread on my bread."

He counted the coins again. He listened to them clink as he dropped them onto the stack. *Tink, tink, tink.* He liked the way the sunlight sparkled on them.

"I'd need to hire farm hands to help plow the fields and pick the produce come harvest time. But I'd not sit lazily in my house and accuse them falsely of sleeping in the field instead of doing a day's work. I'd work the fields right beside them. Then I would know how hard it was and why they did or did not get the plowing done because it was too soon after the rain. But I would pay my workers honest wages, Falstaff. I wouldn't make them live in a smelly barn or a shack with a leaky roof and cracks in the walls that let the weather come through. They'd have a decent house with their own stove for cooking and heating in the wintertime. I would have their respect because I earned it. Not because I have more than they do."

All that had seemed wrong or unfair in his life sashayed before his eyes as he watched the shine of the sun reflect off the coins. He dropped them, one by one.

Tink, tink, tink.

"No, it wouldn't be right, Falstaff. I couldn't take them from him. I hear wizards travel about helping people. You know with plagues, making medicines, and fighting unexplainable evil things. I imagine he needs them for his own food, housekeeping, potion making, and stuff.

Tink, tink, tink.

"Autumn is gone, and folk would not be as likely to hire me with less work to be done. I know I could hunt my food, but grazing would be scarce for you Falstaff. If I could bag a boar or a deer and sell it in a village often enough, I could get you some feed grain."

"Perhaps, I could just borrow some from the old wizard. Maybe just ten coins. It wouldn't harm him. That would be enough to see us through winter. I would leave a note saying I owed him the money."

Tink, tink, tink.

"Well, it still wouldn't be right either because I don't know when I could pay him back and Robert Wayne Thomas is not a thief. I might possibly hire on as a soldier somewhere, only until winter is passed. I'm big enough that if I lie about my age, I could get hired. I don't like the idea of being a lazy soldier. Come spring I could find a farm to work on."

He noticed something strange about the coins. He examined one more closely. Someone had etched tiny symbols along the edge of the coins. Other than that, he thought they looked just like common coins of the realm. He had learned to read a little bit in his travels, but he knew not the meaning of the runes. He placed the coin on the stack and then gathered them into his hands.

"No, it wouldn't be right."

Robert stood and opened the tree. He dropped the coins back into the chest and closed the vault. He started to saddle his horse.

The hawk sailed down to the ground. Suddenly, an orb of light surrounded it. The orb grew to six feet in size and vanished to leave the wizard standing in the clearing.

Robert grabbed his dagger and stepped back a few paces.

"I thought I saw a horse in the brush last night. I'm glad I returned this morning."

"I didn't take anything, your Lordship."

"I know. I've been watching you. Lad, you know not what magically enchanted evil things I hide from the world in this tree. For example, those coins were enchanted by an evil wizard. They allow the giver to have powers over the receiver and can be used to make a person do horrible things, even against his will." The wizard pressed his hand on the tree and spoke the command. He removed the chest of coins.

"Robert, it has taken me decades to gather all the coins the evil wizard enchanted. It is a good thing, even as troubled a life for a lad, down on his luck, such as yourself has endured, you are a good and honest person. I would hate starting over to search for those coins again. Most of people who had the coins never knew of their power. Some learned that dark secret and used them for their own wicked gain. I have not the power to destroy them." He stroked his beard in thought.

"Maybe I should take a voyage far out to sea and drop them overboard in the locked chest. They will never be discovered at the bottom of the ocean. Do know how to handle a sailing boat? I would hire you for an honest wage."

Robert nodded with a smile. "I've sailed a small skiff a time or two, Sir."

"As it happens, I have an aging friend with a small farm and no family to leave it to. He could use a strong and honest young man to work for him. Would you be interested?"

Robert's chest swelled with hope. "Yes, Sir."

"But I need you to promise never to open my tree again."

"That will be the easiest promise I could ever make, Sir."

"Excellent, Robert." The wizard closed the tree, turned, and walked down the trail out of the woods. Robert followed with a spring in his step, trailing Falstaff behind him. He would have a roof over his head for the Yuletide and food for Falstaff after all.

The Christmas Without Presents
By
Kassy Paris

My parents made Christmas a big deal every year, even though money was always tight. In fact, they charged a lot of our Christmas presents and then paid them off for months during the following year. All this of course, we were never told; I deduced it during the years after I realized the truth about Santa.

Speaking of Santa Claus, there were never any presents under our Christmas tree until Christmas morning. All our friends' parents bought, wrapped, and placed their gifts under the tree before Christmas Eve. These kids shook the boxes or peeked through the wrapping paper trying to figure out the contents. One friend went so far as to unwrap his presents with care and put them back together while his parents were out of the house.

Our friends ceased to believe in Santa by the time they were six or seven and tried to convince us Santa was really our parents. We knew they were wrong because Santa always delivered our presents. There was nowhere in our two bedroom house to hide much of anything—four daughters plus three miniscule closets minus an attic and a basement equals no place to hide anything. Santa had to be real.

This particular Christmas I was eleven. Christmas Eve proceeded as usual. Mama and Daddy left the house early in the morning, Mama to buy groceries and gifts for our grandparents and Daddy to his news reporter's beat. When they returned home, we had our traditional chili dinner then were scooted off to bed because Santa would arrive only after we were asleep.

Dawn broke and my sisters and I awoke with it. We crawled out of the double set of bunk beds in our bedroom, shivering against the cold and excitement coursing through our bodies. What did Santa bring us this year? Would we get all of the items on our mile-long lists?

The house was a box divided into four rooms. The bedrooms were on the north side of the house and separated by a hallway and the bathroom. The kitchen and living room were on the south side. Our parents' bedroom had two doors, one to the hallway and one into the living room. The only other way into the living room from our bedroom was through the kitchen, unless we wanted to disturb our parents, which we didn't.

Being the oldest, I led the way, easing open the door to the living room in case Santa had not quite finished his job. We were stair-step children, only six years separated me from the baby, Katrina, with Krissy and Karolyn being jammed between us. At the moment, my three sisters were crowded behind me waiting to catch their first glimpse of the bounty that was Christmas.

I stood frozen in place. I could not believe what my eyes beheld. The Christmas tree stood in the corner, lights blazing brilliant as ever. Not a present could be seen. Instead of dozens of wrapped boxes filling the empty space beneath the tree and spilling out into the room, the floor was bare. My sisters pushed against me, trying to get inside. They squeezed into the room and stood mute when they realized what I had been staring at for long seconds.

"What happened?" Krissy asked. "Where are the presents?"

"I don't know."

"Were we too bad?"

Krissy was always in hot water for something. She was the "bad one."

"I don't know." Karolyn stood with one thumb in her

mouth, eyes wide, and twisted her ponytail with her free hand. Katrina ran across the room and opened Mama's and Daddy's door, no longer concerned about disturbing them. The absence of Christmas presents jumped to the top of our priority lists.

"Daddy, Santa didn't come," Katrina said, almost in tears.

Daddy mumbled and Mama shifted in bed. "Huh?" Daddy asked.

By this time we were all at their door.

"Santa didn't come."

"We didn't get any presents."

All of us talked at once, a cacophony of high-pitched voices disturbing the early morning when "Jingle Bells" should have been ringing out.

Daddy rubbed his face and forced his eyes to open. Slinging off the covers and swinging his feet to the floor, Daddy sat up on the side of the double bed. He reached for his glasses and settled them on his face, lifting his right eyelid and propping it on the brace that followed the curve of the rims. A WWII injury had severed the nerve in his eyelid, causing it to droop closed without his invention.

"What are you talking about? Are you sure? Santa always comes." He stood and looked through the door into the living room.

We backed out of the way and let him step into the room. He stood just inside the door and looked around.

"Well, you're right. There's nothing here." He scratched his head. "I wonder what could have happened?"

I stood silent, waiting. Waiting for Daddy to fix it. Daddy could fix everything.

After another minute or so of listening to the questions and whining, Daddy spoke "I see the problem. I must have forgotten to leave the door unlocked. Santa couldn't get in."

Without a fireplace and chimney, Santa had to come through the front door. A locked door equaled no way inside. My gazed fixed on the big square lock as Daddy took one step, twisted the knob on the lock and the doorknob at the same time, and then pulled the door open.

There, piled on the five-foot square front porch, down the steps leading up to the porch and continuing down the short sidewalk and overflowing onto the frost-covered lawn, were all our presents. Footprints, where the frozen grass had been trampled, glistened in the sunrise.

In the midst of the squeals and shouts, Daddy spoke again. "I knew Santa wouldn't forget you. Get your shoes on and let's get them into the house."

He didn't have to speak twice. We flew out the door and had the dozens of presents in the house in less than five minutes. I don't remember Daddy lifting a finger, just sitting on the couch waiting for Mama to brew a pot of coffee and bring him a cup so we could start the process of ripping into our goodies.

I'll never forget the Christmas of 1962. East Texas was different during that time. Safe. Secure. A place where Santa still existed and the world revolved around our loving family.

Sometimes, I long for the simplicity of that era because today the world seems to spin faster and faster. I can't fly around the world backwards and reverse time like Superman, but I can let my mind transport me back to those days and become filled with the experiences whenever I want. That's almost as good.

Memories of Christmas
By
C. R. Myers

Christmas loomed right around the corner, only two weeks away Mama said. In my seven-year-old mind, fourteen days stood just this side of eternity. School had let out for Christmas vacation, and the chill in the air promised snow.

Daddy took us kids with him to the woods to choose a Christmas tree. I found a beautiful cedar tree, but Daddy said it was too big. My brother and sister were younger and chose trees even larger. Finally, Daddy found a very small tree, which he said would do. I sighed in disappointment because it looked so scrawny. The world's smallest Christmas tree. Surely, this tree would ruin Christmas. But Daddy said it would do just fine. Then, he surprised us even more by taking only the top half. We shook our heads in defeat. Just wait until Mama found out.

Daddy brought the tree inside the house, and something magical happened. It wasn't small any more. In fact, it had grown so big the tiny cedar filled the space, its branches crushed against the window pane, and its top bent over, smashed against the ceiling. I liked it all squashed up like that, but Mama told him to cut off the bottom so the angel would fit. More cutting. She was right, of course. A Christmas tree had to have an angel on top.

Daddy went deep into the hall storage closet and brought out boxes of decorations. First, we strung the lights. Red, blue, orange, and green glowed from inch and a half long bulbs. We'd had the strands through several seasons, and some of the bulbs were scratched so that white light shown through the colors. My favorite bulbs were red with clear tubes of yellow liquid. I never knew what they were supposed to represent, but I loved to watch the bubbles go up and down in the tubes.

Garland, ornaments, and tinsel would follow the lights. Later, Mama helped us cut construction paper to make chains and string popcorn. Sometimes, she bought candy canes for us to hang around the limbs. We loved to turn out the house lights and sit on the living-room rug admiring the beautiful tree.

I loved to watch Mama wrap the presents. She measured and cut the shiny paper for a perfect fit. Her folds, always precise and crisp, made a pleasing finish. My favorite part came next. Mama made the most beautiful bows in the entire world. She looped ribbon around her fingers before making two tiny cuts in the middle. Then, using a short piece of ribbon, she tied a knot between the cuts, twisted the ribbon in well-practiced fashion, and a beautiful bow appeared. She taped one bow to each present in the top left corner and sat the boxes under the tree.

Christmas cooking, however, topped all else. Mama spent hours cooking treats for our big family Christmas celebration. On Christmas Eve, Mama set the table with a huge cut-crystal bowl full of three-layered Jello salad consisting of red Jello, cream cheese with pineapple, and green Jello. Next to that sat the platter of toothpick appetizers, each containing an olive, a slice of Vienna sausage, and a square of cheese. Nuts, chips, and a crock-pot of hot cheese dip covered the end. Homemade cakes and pies, along with Mama's special fudge lined the counter. Pigs-in-a-Blanket waited patiently by the stove for their turn in the oven.

The *pièce de résistance*, however, had to be Mama's homemade enchiladas. Mama and Daddy, working side by side, spent a couple of hours browning the meat and onions, preparing the sauce, and frying the tortillas for the enchiladas. After carefully stuffing each tortilla, they placed the finished shells together on a cookie sheet, covered them with sauce and cheese, and baked them. Yummy. I was never sure how the Mexican dish became a part of our Christmas, but I was sure glad it had.

Once, the food was ready, grandparents on both sides of the family began to arrive with presents to place under the tree. Experience had taught us kids that our gifts would consist of underwear and school clothes. I never thought of us as poor. We always had enough to eat and a roof over our heads. If we got a toy, which we always did, it would come from Santa, and he wouldn't arrive until almost midnight.

Stuffed and giddy with excitement, I disappeared upstairs to peek through the living room windows. Pressed against the cool glass, I squinted into the darkness to spot the distant glow of car lights. Presents waited to be opened until my aunt arrived from Austin. She and my uncle drove the two hundred miles every Christmas Eve to be with us. What a treat. My aunt arrived looking like a movie star, arms full of store-wrapped presents. We knew they contained unimagined treasure. She handed me a small box wrapped in red velvet, a gold necklace with a single pearl. And it was real. I felt very special.

A noise upstairs caught my attention. Was it Santa? We lived in a split-level house. While we were visiting downstairs, Santa would deliver gifts upstairs beneath the tree—a hobby-horse for my brother, and a western-style toy gun with a holster—a dolly that drank and wet for my sister, which she invariably named "Susie"—a Barbie doll for me with a carrying box.

I loved that Barbie doll. She had fluffy blonde hair and a bright blue dress. I didn't know she was really a Midge doll, bought at a half-price sale. To me, she was perfect, just as Christmas was perfect.

I treasure my memories of Christmas. The traditions my parents created and made special wove a rich tapestry against which to build our lives. The detailed repetitions they honored year after year provided us with a profound sense of who we were and defined our family group.

Many Christmas seasons have come and gone since those days. We kids are grown now and have kids and grandkids of our own. We try to make their Christmas times special, enriched with traditions from our family past as well as new traditions all our own. We bring rich food and brightly wrapped presents, but most of all we bring them love. We hope they'll remember the season with fondness and warmth. We hope that one day they'll say, "I remember Christmas," and Christmas memories will bubble forth and fill their hearts with joy.

Shadowlon
By
Larence Shaddox

A cloaked figure stood as he observed the camp of circled wagons from his hiding spot in the shadows of the trees. Snow covered the earth all around the country. In the center of the circle of wagons burned the main fire. Beside it a woman stood with her head down.

The violin player drew his bow slowly, coaxing a haunting, beautiful tone.

The woman allowed the music from the violin to set the mood. Singing softly, she slowly raised her head. Her beautiful voice was as captivating as the tune of the violin. She sang an old ballad of a Golden Knight named Shadowlon.

Each legendary knight traveled the land, accompanied only by his shadow. They protected the common people and forced bad overlords to amend their ways and be fairer to their serfs. Shadowlon made the mistake of falling in love with a king's young bride-to-be and the king had a great wizard cast a curse upon him. Shadowlon roamed the country alone, seeking redemption.

As the woman sang, she glanced about the camp at her companions and beyond. For a brief moment, her wandering eye gazed directly at the figure in the shadows.

The warrior held his horse's reins close to the bridle and gently stroked its muzzle to keep it quiet. When the woman finished her song, cheers and clapping rang from all around the camp.

"Bravo! Willowmina, never have I heard you sing with such feeling," spoke out a heavyset man.

Willowmina stepped over and whispered into his ear.

The man stood and walked to the center of the camp.

"Hello, Stranger," the man said as he peered beyond the light into the darkness. "I am Willitar. Please come in from the dark winter's night and join us by the fire. We are a family clan. We have bread and stew to ward off the cold."

The cloaked figure grasped his crossbow and removed it from the saddle horn. He held the weapon behind him to hide it.

Suddenly, several men came out of the shadows from between the wagons across the camp from the warrior. They were a ragged looking group, wearing soiled clothes. Each man carried a long sword drawn and ready. Screams and shouts erupted, but no weapon was lifted against the bandits as they herded the four men along with thirty women and children into the center of the camp. The bandits numbered seven.

"What do you want from us?" Willitar shouted.

"We will have your riches."

"We are a simple folk, living in wagons. We only have the riches of health from a simple, clean living. We have but a few coins in the entire camp."

The leader of the bandits was the largest man in the group, standing over six feet tall. "You have livestock, provisions, and a pretty lark to entertain us with her songs." He stepped near Willowmina and looked her over with an appraising eye.

"You would leave us with nothing? As for my daughter, I'll see you in Hell first."

"That can be arranged, old man." The bandit raised his sword.

It was then that the cloaked figure led his horse into the camp, stopping at the edge of the light. He shook the bridle, and his horse snorted. At just shy of six feet and dressed in a dark cloak draped over his extensive shoulders with his broadsword strapped to his back, all attention in the camp turned to him.

"I am most gracious for your kind offer of food and the warmth of your fire, Sir. You are good people to be so kind to strangers. I think it is a pity that vagabonds are about the land and would take kindness for weakness and choose to rob you." His deep, mellow voice rang out across the camp.

"Who are you?" The leader shouted.

"Did you not hear the song? I am a Shadowlon."

"Well, ghost warrior of childhood legends, as you can see, this is my camp now. You are not welcome. Leave."

"That will be difficult because I cannot stand witness and allow your crimes. Throw down your weapons, run off to the filthy swamp that you snakes crawled out of, and I'll let you live."

The vagabond leader laughed. "We have you out numbered, seven to one. We can kill you and still take our needs from this clan."

"Not when you are dead."

"Really now? Johan, Martall, kill him!"

Two men started running from the far side of the camp toward him. The warrior released the reins, stepping away from his horse as he swung his crossbow out and raised it waist high. His steps positioned him so that the bandits were running one behind the other. He fired the crossbow level at the first one. The quarrel was made for combat. Destructive to the internal organs, it went completely through the first man and sank deeply into the second one. Both bandits dropped to their knees gasping for breath as they fell over to die in mere seconds.

"Stones and clubs kill as well as arrows and swords," the warrior said as he cast aside his crossbow. He pulled the cord at his neck to remove his cloak with his left hand as he drew the sword with his right. He was dressed in full chain mail for battle. Across his chest, woven into the silver mail, were golden links forming a dragon.

"Your odds are down by two. Run now or die."

"That wasn't very sporting, Ghost," the leader snarled. "Now you have no more quarrels. Fokan, Somat, Hemdel! Kill him!"

Three bandits standing abreast rushed the warrior together.

He cast his cloak into the face of the man on the left. Then he knocked away the other two blades and stepped in to punch the center man squarely in the nose with a gauntlet-covered fist. The punch sent the bandit staggering backwards. The warrior swung his blade and killed the man he had fouled with his cloak. The man on the right turned, his inertia carrying him past the warrior, in time to face his death as he was gutted by a forceful swing of the broadsword. The warrior turned and jabbed his sword into the chest of the man he had punched. They stared at each other a moment as the man's eyes glazed over, and he fell backward off the sword. The warrior stepped over the bodies toward the leader.

"There were seven, then five and now only two."

The leader ran at him, screaming, as he swung his sword in a high arc, in an attempt to chop the warrior's head off.

The knight raised his sword, blocked, and forced the blade away. He met the man's body with a thrust from his shoulder. The larger man's weight did nothing in his attempt to knock the knight over. The knight swung at the bandit's mid-section. The bandit jumped back and parried the swing well. The knight swung his blade down and to his rear in an arc to cleave the bandit from the top as he stepped forward. The bandit raised his long sword to block the swing. The weight of the broad sword, combined with the force the knight put behind it, was too much for the bandit's lighter sword and arm position. The mighty sword sliced through the collarbone and the first two ribs of the bandit. He staggered backwards. The knight was raising his sword for a killing thrust, when he saw the bandit receive a crashing blow to the side of the head from a double-fist-sized rock. The bandit collapsed on the spot and the knight stood looking at the face of an angry Willowmina. He looked about to see the last man being beaten down by the men and women with rocks and pieces of firewood as clubs.

"I hoped you would take my meaning. Thank you for your help."

She smiled. "It is we who should thank you, Golden Knight."

The knight sheathed his sword and retrieved his cloak and crossbow.

"Yes," Willitar said, "how can we repay you? We have little, but the stew is good."

"There is no need. The lovely song was payment enough," the warrior said as he mounted his horse.

"Please, stay and have some food at least." Willitar held out his hand.

The knight removed his gauntlet and accepted the out-stretched hand. The knight saw shock in Willitar at how cold his hand was.

"Thank you for your offer, but I have already eaten today."

The warrior reached into a pouch hanging from his saddle horn. He leaned over and gave Willowmina a large, beautiful, yellow rosebud.

"Show this to the guards at the toll gate tomorrow, and you will be given tax-free passage papers across the kingdom."

"What name should we call you, Golden Knight?"

He smiled sweetly at her and said softly, "You sang my song tonight." The knight turned his horse and trotted off.

Willowmina broke the spell of silence. "Bless you, Good Knight! We will pray for your redemption, Shadowlon!"

Man and horse faded from existence before they left the light of the fire.

'Tis the Season

Spring

The Easter Bunny's Gift
by
C. R. Myers

In the still of the morning before the dawn,
Before the squirrel's chatter and the robin's song,
While the sun is still sleeping and the flowers are closed,
The Easter Bunny's tying Easter bows.

He wears a white waistcoat
And a pink bowtie.
His shirt is pale yellow.
His pants match the sky.

While you're in your beds all snuggled and warm
In the dewdrop time on Easter morn,
The Easter Bunny goes hop, hop, hop
Hiding Easter eggs and chocolate drops.

Red eggs, orange eggs, purple, and blue
Eggs for me and eggs for you
Suckers, lemon drops, and marshmallow threats
The Bunny brings presents and good things to eat.

He tiptoes through gardens and climbs over walls.
He hides in the treetops where Whip-poor-wills call.
You never will see him; he's quick and he's fast.
He'll hide all the goodies before dawn has past.

And when you awaken, wipe the sleep from your eyes.
Grab your Easter basket to find your surprise.
Look under the Bluebells and Forget-Me-Nots,
Under Buttercups, Tulips, and clay flowerpots.

'Tis the Season

Fill your basket with candies and Easter eggs, yes.
For Bunny is hiding; he's watching your quest.
Find all of his treasures and his little gifts too
For it's his way of saying, "Happy Easter to You."

By the Sweat of the Brow
By
Brinda Carey

The engine breathed the force of the living,
No sound save the green beast he rides alone.
Grateful to God for health and chores given
To provide his family food and a home.
He plows rough, callused fingers through his hair,
Wipes the sweat from his brow, and then he sighs.
Great clouds of red dust swirl in the thick air
And with faith he cries out that he relies
On the Lord not to leave him toiling earth
'Til the day his worn body crumbles apart.
Yet he plows on to give seeds place of birth-
Worshiping God for the peace in his heart.
In a field of graves, he makes one last round
Awaiting his own rebirth from the ground.

Kat and the Cougar
By
Jeannie Faulkner Barber

Case Devereaux's hand caressed the small of my back, warm against the bareness revealed by my low-cut, short, amber dress. As a redhead, I love a brazen color scheme, and Case loves for us to stand out in a crowd. *Ah, this is the anniversary of the day we met, the first day of Spring, and I intend for it to be a night my husband won't soon forget.*

He took my sable jacket and checked it. "Please put it under Katarina Devereaux." He rolled the 'r' as he pronounced our last name.

I smiled and adjusted the long strand of white pearls he had given me earlier.

The girl behind the counter dropped her pen. "Uh, yes sir."

His wavy blond hair and rugged jaw line made me quiver. "What a lovely surprise to dine here tonight, Case." I looked into his azure eyes. "I've heard the Red Everest has a five-star rating."

"Five stars can't compare to the woman on my arm tonight." He touched a long curl on my shoulder and let his hand linger. "The blonde streaks you added remind me of a calico kitten."

I pretended to purr while my eyes surveyed his body. A white tuxedo shirt outlined the ripple of sculpted biceps. Unbuttoned, rolled-up sleeves revealed blond hair on his tanned arms as he draped a tailored jacket over one shoulder. His black jeans fit perfectly, all the way down to…black ostrich cowboy boots. *Yum.*

The maître d' gestured. "Right this way, please."

We made our way into the mainstream of the restaurant. Mirrored columns divided the dining room into semi-private squares. Above each section, brass Concho-shaped fixtures emitted a plume of golden rays. Pomegranate brocade covered the chairs and graced tables topped with sheer white voile. A small bouquet of lavender, black dahlias, and pink roses sat in a fluted vase on each one, and vapory lighting beneath the opaque floor cast a subtle glow.

The maître d' led us to a table by a concave window. The spring skyline of Ft. Worth glittered before me. An incandescence below spread toward the thick ebony flatland approaching the bountiful ranch owned by the Devereaux family. *Old money.*

Case pulled out my chair. I laid down the beaded bag, slid my legs under the table, and let the tip of my bronze high-heels travel slightly up his leg when he sat across from me.

He gave me a wink and grabbed my hand.

The waiter offered a leather-bound list. "Would you like to order some wine?"

"A white Chardonnay dated this month, 2010," Case said.

"But of course," the waiter replied and disappeared.

"Did I tell you how gorgeous you look tonight, Kat?" He squeezed my hand.

"Only a dozen times on the way here, but who's counting?"

We dined on duck breast in cherry sauce with snow peas and ginger peach sorbet for dessert. The delectable food was secondary to the attention I received from my adoring admirer.

As we poured the last of the wine, and toasted 'to us' again, the waiter handed Case back his credit card. "Might I lead the way for you and your lady, sir?

"Thank you." Case stood up. "Ready to work off

some of those calories?"

I raised an eyebrow. "Night over so soon?"

He laughed. "Dancing is what I had in mind, but we can skip it if you like." His hand rested at my elbow as we entered the elevator and ascended to the rooftop floor.

"Where are we going?" I cooed in his ear.

When the elevator stopped, the door slid open. A few steps away stood a man in a black suit, dark glasses, and felt fedora—my summation of what a secret service agent must look like. His arms were crossed over his chest and behind him was a double-mirrored door. I caught a glimpse of our reflection. *Damn, we look good together.*

Case cast a slight wave of his hand, and the 'agent' opened the door.

Inside, a band, the size of a philharmonic orchestra, hammered out rock tunes from the '80's while couples boogied on the dance floor. The parquet floor had a unique Aztec design and was like walking on ice. The contoured fresco ceiling gave an impression of billowy pink clouds as rose-colored crystals dangled from a dozen or more chandeliers.

Case pulled me into his arms. "I can't wait to show you off."

The woodsy aroma of his cologne gave me a heady sensation, and I pressed my body closer to him.

Dance after dance, he twirled me around the floor until the other couples stepped back and gave us the entire space. He tenderly placed his lips on mine then lifted me into his arms before he dipped me low to the floor and back. To my delight, he stepped sideways and bowed. Raw emotion and adrenalin made my heart thud in my chest when applause erupted from the crowd.

I must be in heaven, right? But…no, what? Is someone talking to *my* man? I blinked my eyes, lifting my mascara-laden lashes as wide as possible as a woman stepped in front of my handsome husband. *Has she lost her mind? Tonight is about us—or better yet, me! What did she just say?*

I stared at the back of a tall, slender woman with bleached-blonde hair dressed in a short, red skirt and jacket. From my view, if her skirt were any tighter, she would have to paint it on.

"Uh, no ma'am, I'm not," Case replied.

I elbowed my way around the intruder. "Excuse me? You're not what, Case?" I tossed my long hair away from my face.

"This lady, uh, I don't think I've had the pleasure of knowing your name," Case said.

"Rosalind…Rosalind Choogar," she said, eyes locked on my date.

"Yes, uh, Ms. Choogar wanted to know if I was a dance instructor, Katarina."

"Choogar, huh? What is that…Russian for cougar?" I planted my hands on my hips and stared at each obvious Botox-injected wrinkle on her face.

The woman clasped her hands together in a patty-cake fashion and laughed. "You're little friend is so funny. I was only hoping this young man was a dance instructor so I might receive a lesson from him."

It was at this point I noticed her cleavage. *I'm gonna puke right down the front of your fake boob job.* I took a deep breath and puffed out my chest (mine are real, by the way). I felt my claws sharpen (after all, my name *is* Kat), and my hand raise slightly when it dawned on me I could beat this woman at her own game.

"Well, Rosie, I'm his *wife* and no, he's not a dance instructor. However, *I* am, and I'd love to teach you a few steps. Shall we?" I pointed toward the dance floor.

The entire room, including the band, appeared to hang on my next word.

"My name is *not*, Rosie. It's Rosalind," my new nemesis insisted.

"Katarina," Case began. "What're you doing?" He shook his head.

I whispered in his ear, "If the lady wants a *lesson*, a lesson she will get." I hurried over to the band and returned with a wide grin on my face. "Okay, Rosie, time to rock and roll."

"Uh, what?"

Without hesitation, I grabbed her arm and shuffled her backwards to the tune of 'Hernando's Hideaway.' From one twist and turn to another, I jetted her across the slick floor like a brand new buffing machine on rent for the weekend. She coughed, gasped, and tried to free herself from my tight rein only to be twirled and flipped in a different direction. Each downbeat of the music gave me more inspiration to treat her to a free dance lesson. After all, wasn't that what she wanted?

I'm sure the song would have continued a few bars longer, but Rosie twisted her ankle, and someone called the 'agent' to carry her away.

Once I smoothed down my cute amber dress and shook my hair off my shoulders, I approached Case, his face plastered with a crescent smile. "Care to dance, sir?" I extended my hand.

He rubbed his jaw. "Man, if I didn't know better, I'd say you were jealous."

"Me? Moi? Don't tease me so, my darling. I merely needed to make the boundary lines crystal clear for dishwater-blonde Rosie," I replied, defiant.

Case whisked me up into his arms, and the crowd began to applaud once more. "I love you, Kat."

I wrapped my arms around his neck. "I love you, too, Case. Just so you know, that's what happens when a cougar tangles with a Kat, and to think, I did it all in five inch stilettos."

The Easter Gift
A True Story
By
C. R. Myers

Mother never liked to sew. Her long, slender fingers were better suited to tripping across the ivories than threading a needle. She learned, of course, because her mother worked as a professional seamstress. I remember my grandmother coming home, making dinner, and sewing until time for bed. She made machine quilts and curtains, as well as clothes for herself, my mother, and us three kids. For Easter, Grandmother would make my mother, my sister, and me matching Easter dresses.

As my grandmother's sewing days slowed, my mother took up the slack. During my middle school and high school years, my mother made my sister and me tent dresses for school, shorts for camp, and Easter dresses for church. My mother sewed well, but I realized even then that sewing frustrated her, always seeming more of a chore than a pleasure.

However, my mother never complained, and we were always dressed well. I remember the weekly trips to the fabric shops filled with bolts of beautiful material and the strong smell of the dye. I remember Mom picking out material for our school and church dresses. After I began to sew, she would let me pin on the pattern and cut out the material. After forty years, I can still see some of those dresses in my mind's eye.

Easter was an especially busy time around our house. Both Mom and Dad sang in the adult choir at church, and we kids sang in the youth choir. The holidays were filled with lots of practice, lots of shopping, lots of cooking, and lots of sewing.

One Easter holiday seemed particularly hectic, and I noticed Mother spending more time than usual at the sewing machine. I noticed because, as I mentioned before, sewing was not my mom's favorite activity.

A few days before Easter Sunday, Mom asked me to run an errand with her. We drove out to the Salvation Army and parked the car. Mom reached into the back and removed two new Easter dresses. I recognized the material. This had been the project she had been working on the last couple of weeks.

"What are those for?" I asked her as we walked to the building.

"My Sunday School class is making Easter dresses for needy kids. I received the measurements for two girls and made the dresses. They will be here to try them on."

I couldn't believe it. My mom had volunteered to make clothes.

We went inside, and Mom explained who we were to the woman behind the counter. The silver-haired matron left and came back with two little girls. The girls smiled shyly, eyes on the new dresses. The matron made the introductions and left with the girls and the dresses.

In only a few minutes, the young ladies re-appeared—smiles stretched across their small faces. They had been transformed by a few yards of organza and lace into Easter Cinderellas.

The matron thanked Mom, and the girls joined in. Mother smiled back, seemingly pleased.

We never spoke about the incident again, and I don't even know if anyone in the family ever knew what my mother had done. But I never forgot. I would always remember how my mother sacrificed her time and talents to make Easter dresses for two needy children. Her gift had been a true labor of love.

Traveling Sands
By
Judith Victoria Douglas

How long had I been walking, checking for landmarks? It Seemed like hours. I finally gave up. I was lost.

Not a good thing in a forest anytime, but especially not nice if it's the one behind your own house.

So, how did this happen?

Day dreaming. Thinking. I walked to relax and unravel a bit on the story I was writing.

I know my way. I should be home by now. Where's that dog?

"Pilot!"

No answer. No sound.

Verging on tears with growing fear, I sat on a stump to figure this out.

My stump!

Circles. That's it. I'm walking in circles.

As I rose to gain a path I should know, I kicked a small bottle among the spring brambles, almost covered by old brown leaves.

What's this, the bottle of sand I lost? Given to me by that old gypsy woman...said 'good luck,' and laughed.

"Humph." Still couldn't remove the cork so, shrugging, I slammed it against my stump.

At first I thought it didn't break. I held it up to look closer. A tiny trickle of minuscule grains popped out as if alive and wanting escape. As a few touched me, I felt a tingle. The light around me changed and the breeze swirled into an encircling gale. A rainbow of sparkling lights surrounded me. I closed my eyes.

Looking up, opening one eye at a time, I was much more lost than I had imagined. I was sitting on a rock in a desert oasis surrounded by camels.

Petrified with fear, I closed my eyes once more and vigorously shook the little bottle, grains sprinkling me, tingling again.

Opening my eyes I saw a beach, clear turquoise waves lapping at my feet. Panic set in

"Awww!"

I shook again, holding my breath. I felt another slight twinge and a sudden cold. I was afraid to open my eyes.

"Pilot!"

Shivering in silence I peeked. Snow—all down the mountain!

Franticly, I shook the bottle again. Another tingle.

"Woof!"

My eyes popped open.

There stood the cottage, my dog at the gate.

"Yes, that's how I'll write it—traveling sands."

Summer

Wanna Take a Swim?
By
Jeannie Faulkner Barber

The warm spring sun beats down, while I walk along the pond.
I watch the waves move out, and it beckons to respond.
A breeze blows my blonde hair, and I kick the sandy beach.
Do I take the dare? There's no one here but me.

Something drops into the water; I look upward and see,
Nothing there but acorns and emerald hand-shaped leaves.
My silly imagination is running wild once more.
I boldly take a few steps closer to the silt-lined shore.

The water's edge reflects all the colors of the sky.
I strip off all my clothes and I take a dip inside.
The ripples ruffle outward and goose bumps start to rise
As I let out all my breath, and the bubbles go awry.

My feet and legs move fast before minnows start to nibble,
And the groan of a bullfrog makes me want to tremble.
"Not today old man, I'm free and I'm alive."
I dip down once again, and I open wide my eyes.

The pondweed twists and bows like a native hula dancer
Swaying back and forth in the cool and soothing azure,
I reach down and hunt for a treasure buried there
Is it a rock, or is it gold, or do I even care?

A few more inches down and maybe, I can reach it,
But the current grabs my body like a black-masked bandit.
My lungs burn with fire as I fight the water monster.
Farther down I go, my heart will surely falter.

Then out of nowhere, I find strength like a warrior

'Tis the Season

Headed into battle, encased in shining armor.
Plunging to the top, away from all of this,
No more to be engulfed in the cavernous abyss.

I spit out all the water and breathe in good fresh air,
Climb up on the bank, only to find my clothes aren't there!
The bullfrog croaks again. I splash him 'til he's soaked.
Shake my fist and say, "So you think that it's a joke?"

Off the lily pad, he jumped onto the shore,
Into the woods so thick, I can't see him any more.
Just like a newborn babe, I stand here in the nude.
If I can't find my clothes, I guess that I'm just screwed.

The chatter up a tree makes me turn, my temper flare.
A squirrel now has my blouse, my shorts, and flying thru the air.
The summer sun beats down as I walk naked by the pond,
And all that I can say is—I guess that I was conned.

Joshua's Tree
By
Gay Ingram

Andy Jones gave another poke with his trowel. "That should help you, Aunt Mary." A glance at a nearby wisteria tree set his mind remembering his wife's funeral. He let out a deep sigh; the children had all been here when he planted it in her honor. "It sure is lonely without her but I think she'd like my choosing that tree for her."

"Who you talking to?"

Andy's heart did a flip-flop. The unexpectedness of the sound surprised him. He thought himself alone. Looking past his shoulder, all he saw at first were two small feet shod in purple plastic flip-flops, a shocking shade of purple. His gaze traveled upward past skinny white legs disappearing under pink shorts and across a giant Barney decorating a green tee-shirt. His look met two eyes set in a child's face whose small red mouth was puckered into an "o." An unruly head-full of short russet curls capped the serious-looking face.

"And where did you come from, young lady?" he asked as he eased his old bones from their cramped position to a comfortable sprawl. He looked all around but saw no adult in sight.

The child had appeared like the legendary leprechauns but bore them no resemblance.

"Well, Mommy said I could go outside as long as I stayed in the back yard. Is this the back yard?"

Her question amused him and he chuckled before replying. "Well, it's my back yard, but you can visit anytime." Then he remembered the moving van unloading its contents the previous day.

"I'll bet you're my new neighbor, aren't you?"

"This is my new house," she replied. "I never lived in a whole house before...one all to myself. And, I never had a back yard before, either." Without pausing to take a breath, she went on, "Whatcha doing in the dirt? Do you like to play in the dirt? Mommy gets mad when I get dirty."

The rush of sentences came like a runaway train, overwhelming Andy. It'd been years since he'd had a conversation with a child. He had grown accustomed to the companionship of silence.

The child continued, undisturbed by the lack of answers. "I have a baby brother. Do you have any family?"

"Well, actually this is my family," he answered, making a wide sweeping motion.

She stood quietly, a puzzled look on her face.

"Like, right here," he explained as he pointed to the bush in front of him, "I was just giving Aunt Mary's roses a boost of fertilizer. She's been kind of drooping, you see." He turned and broke off one of the pink buds and offered it to the child.

"Aunt Mary, meet...I don't believe I know your name," he said.

"I'm Samantha and my brother is Jonathan. Then, there's Mommy and Daddy...but Daddy don't live with us anymore so we had to leave the city and move here. Why do you call the flower Aunt Mary?" she asked with a sudden change of subject.

"Well, because when my Aunt Mary was a young lady she married a man who took her to live far across the country. The day she left, we planted this rose bush."

"Oh."

"Over there is my Lillian's wisteria tree and beside it is Joshua's oak tree." Something in his voice made the girl look closely into his face.

"Why are you sad?"

He paused before answering. "Because Joshua went away to war and never came back."

"Samantha...Sam, where are you?" a voice called out.

"Here I am, Mommy, in the back yard." A grownup version of Samantha, baby propped on her hip, appeared from behind the hedge.

"But what are you doing over there?" she asked, "And why are you bothering that nice man?"

"I was just 'sploring my back yard," Samantha answered. "The man was 'splaining about his family."

Andy pushed himself up from the ground and crossed the short distance to the young woman.

"You must be Samantha's mother," he said, holding out his hand. "I'm your neighbor, Andy Jones. Welcome to Redbird Circle."

She gave him a smile that seemed to encase Andy in sunshine as she reached out to take his hand.

"I apologize if my daughter has disturbed you," she said. "We've always lived in a city apartment house and she doesn't understand about property lines."

"No problem. No problem at all," Andy quickly reassured her. "I live alone now. My wife died last year and all the children are gone. So, visitors are welcome, even the little ones." He looked toward Samantha and smiled.

"Well, if she's ever a bother..." the woman's voice trailed off as she looked about the lush yard. She let out a gasp of delight.

"You must have a green thumb, like they say in the magazines," she said, "your yard is lovely."

Her enthusiasm embarrassed Andy and he looked into the distance to hide his pleasure. "Well, not really; I just have a lot of time to look after my family."

Samantha's mother tilted her head and waited for an explanation.

He shrugged his shoulders before going on. "I was just introducing Samantha to my family," he said with a motion toward the area behind him, "Would you like to meet them, too?"

"I'd be delighted." Her voice held a note of expectancy. "This is a new experience for me and I know I have a lot to learn...about growing things, I mean." There was a pause as she considered her next question. "But, why do you refer to them as your family?"

"Well, ever since my parents came to live in this house, they had this custom of adding a special plant whenever someone in the family experienced some major event. After they died, my wife and I just continued. Now, I may be living all by myself but I still have "my family" nearby."

"What a lovely idea," she murmured. While they spoke, Samantha stood nearby looking from one face to another during the long conversation. Now she tugged at her mother's jeans.

"Come on, Mommy, let's go meet Joshua's tree and the rest of the family."

Trowel in hand, Andy led the way, smiling to himself. *Sometimes God has a strange way of answering the prayers of an old man. Looks like I won't be lonely anymore.*

Cowboy Philosophy
By
Denny L. Youngblood

Uncle Max loved his big red truck better than me. I know because he told me so.

"Boy, I've only known you fer fifteen years. So, don't go messin' with my truck. Ya hear me, boy?"

Though the words changed a little each time, it was basically the same old speech I had heard once a week now for the past three months. Uncle Max was old; the big red rig was old, so why shouldn't the speech be old also?

Mom pawned me off on him for the summer so I would learn some morals and the value of money. Although I was young, I could still rattle off a handful of relatives we both knew with more values than Uncle Max. It was like learning to play baseball from a ballet teacher.

Don't get me wrong; Uncle Max possessed a few morals—just as many as reality television programs showed us each week. A tattered, sun-bleached covered New Testament sat beside a huge overflowing ashtray on the cracked, weathered vinyl dash. The rubber band holding the sacred text together looked as if the dried, parched elastic would snap if it you looked at wrong.

"That there's God's Word, boy. Do you good to know what He's gotta say 'bout you."

The first time he said that, I sheepishly leaned over to take a peek and see just what God did have to say about me. That's when Uncle Max slapped the puddin' right out of me.

"That's God's Word, boy. Ain't yours. I'm paying you enough so you can git your own."

Mile after lonesome mile, the little Testament sat there. Uncle Max never touched it. Sometimes he would scoot it over some after emptying and replacing the ashtray. For the most part, the searing rays blasting through the windshield was the only thing that bothered it.

I knew better than to ask questions. As sure as Momma named me Billy Joe Wilkins, I knew that asking questions of Uncle Max would not be in my best interest, but I needed to hear a live human voice. I could only handle so much of Reba and The Possum before something inside of me broke loose. MegaDeath was being replaced by the Dixie Chicks. As George sang about being a fireman, Pearl Jam eased quietly into my memory.

"Uncle Max, how do you know what God's Word says? I mean, does He really talk about me in that little book?"

He never looked at me eye to eye. It was more like he stared right through me, talking to some unknown entity on the other side of me, somewhere beyond the cab, residing among the billions of wooden sticks used for fence posts along the county road. It gave me a weird feeling as though he was looking in one ear and out the other.

"God don't like nincompoops, boy, and you're sure 'nuff walking a thin line." Uncle Max gazed right through me as he lit another Camel. I sure hoped his other eye was watching the road.

"I know what that book says 'cause God tells me what's in it. And yep, you're sure as snot in there, boy. Somewhere in Romans or Italians, 'round the third chapter, I think."

Perhaps I am a nincompoop because as much as I hated it, I could feel another question chomping at the bits, waiting to get out. "So, what did God say about me?"

The Camel disappeared in three long cough-filled drags as he added the squashed filter to his growing collection of other flat butts. Faith Hill was crooning about being kissed when I lowered my window to let the cloud of smoke escape. His eyes roamed back to the long dotted line in the middle of the highway.

"God says you're going to Hell in a hand basket, boy."

Well, that certainly answered my question. No beating around the bush with Uncle Max around.

"Now then, if you were to change your ways, then maybe God would see something good in you and save your scrawny hide."

My eyes widened a bit. Hell may not be my only option after all. "So, what is it I need to change, Uncle Max? I'm only fifteen and this is my first real summer job. Damn, I can't even get Missy Ann to kiss me!"

A line of invisible fire shot from his eyes toward me. "You'd better quit your cussin' in my truck, boy. God don't like a filthy mouth. Reckon that's why my sister talked me into totin' you along this summer. You are driving her whacko with all your hormones wanting Missy Ann and all. God don't like that none a 'tall. I would give my life fer my truck, boy, but you're only here 'cause in a moment of weakness, your momma caught me off guard."

Since Garth had some friends in low places, I thought sure I would be more welcome with them than here with Uncle Max. I didn't think he actually hated me because I was sure God would probably thump him on the head for that. Yet, Uncle Max made it plenty clear that I would probably never get a Christmas card from him.

"Anyways, like I was saying before you got me off track, you need to change your ways, boy. Change 'em up right quick-like 'cause God is gonna drop on in out of them clouds there." He squinted and thrust a brown, nicotine-stained finger toward the gunmetal-gray sky. "And tote you on down to Hell so you can play hopscotch with the devil."

I once saw my baby sister, Alicia, play hopscotch, and I felt certain this was not going to be very entertaining, devil or no devil. However, Uncle Max was on a roll now, and I was anxious to hear what else old Mr. Devil had in store for me.

"Some things in life are more important than others, you know. Take Missy Ann, for example. No matter how many butterflies your belly gets whenever you think about her, she ain't near as important as you gittin' a proper education. You git in there and learn them three R's right good-like, and pretty soon you can be making honest money to support you and Missy Ann."

"But Uncle Max, I don't want to marry her. I just want to kiss her."

"Uh-huh, and just as soon as you two start swapping spit, she's gonna whisper in your ear, you'll lose your dang mind, and 'fore long you two will have a yard full of young'uns and wonder how you got into that mess. For every hundred bucks a month you got coming in, you'll have a hundred twenty going out."

I'll admit that eighth grade algebra is a bit tricky, but somehow the formula for success did not seem to include spending twenty dollars more per month than what I have. Then the nincompoop began rising in me again and another dumb question bubbled up.

"So, if you have more money going out than you have coming in, is that why you always run on seventeen tires instead of eighteen?"

"Good question there, boy," Uncle Max blurted out.

Now, I knew I should not have asked.

"You see, now you're startin' to think like me."

Oh God, I think I would rather dance a jig with the devil than to think like Uncle Max.

"There are several laws at work here, boy. First, you have your law of physics. Now that law says I can run seventeen as good as eighteen and save myself the price of one tire. Dang good law, that one is. Then there's the law of supply and demand. Another good 'un. That law says until there's a demand fer me to slap on more tread, then I don't need to supply it. Yep, dang good laws, them are."

Naïve fifteen year olds, two months shy of sixteen, are not well versed in law. I never read a law book in my life, never really saw one, yet I felt a nagging tug that these were not actual laws written down in a prized book somewhere. They sounded more like Uncle Max's wild brand of cowboy philosophy.

"Is there a law for the log book we're supposed to write in also?"

"Yeah there's a law! Boy, you're sharp as a tack today. That one's called the Writ of has-been Corpses. Figure the best time to scribble in it is when I am dead-to-the-bone, dog-tired. That's where the corpses come in."

"So, if I were to change my ways, be more like you, Uncle Max, then maybe the old devil might go find somebody else to play hopscotch with?"

"Mercy boy." Uncle Max said as he wiped at a tear. "You know how to say the nicest things to an old man. Change your ways, figure out what God wants you to do with yourself, and study them laws. You'll do just fine." A billowing cloud of blue-gray smoke boiled around him and his Camels.

I sat back in the thick, acrid smoke and tried to envision my life at forty. Pot-bellied, an old stained straw hat, sitting behind the wheel of Uncle Max's big red rig, dispensing age-old morals and values to my own nephew.

"Uncle Max, when you retire, are you going to leave me your rig?"

It was as though Reba and Garth stopped dead in their tracks, silent—waiting for him to speak.

"Boy, I've owned this rig since before you were a smile on your daddy's face, and I've only known you fer 'bout fifteen years. Ya ain't gittin' my truck. Ya hear me, boy?"

Grandma's Cactus Garden
By
Brinda Carey

The pain in my chest grew stronger in my attempt to stifle a sob. Only fitting that I felt a small portion of what Grandma must have felt when her heart decided that eighty-six years was long enough to pump without rest. The sound of people sniffing, crying, and coughing grated on my nerves. How unfair that I was still expected to be the strong one and remain in control when all I wanted to do was crawl under a quilt and cry.

I hung my head in prayer, asking God to comfort and strengthen me. With eyes still closed, I took a deep breath and smiled at the memory evoked from the smell of freshly turned earth and the sound of Aunt Carol, who was sitting behind me, humming "Amazing Grace".
*

Grandma's quilt gave me the best hug I'd had in a long time. I snuggled deeper into the colorful girls wearing bonnets while I soaked up the heavenly smell of coffee and bacon. I was only nine and not allowed to drink coffee, but I could almost taste it just by breathing in the scent. Most days at home Momma shuffled out peanut butter sandwiches or cinnamon toast like a deck of cards as my five brothers and sisters and I rushed to meet the bus for school. However, Grandma always cooked a big breakfast. We would need it to accomplish all the work to be done. In 1969, everyone in west Texas had a garden and Grandma was no exception.

"Rise and shine," Grandma hollered from the kitchen. "Wake up sleepy head."

The linoleum floor was uncommonly chilly for a

bright spring morning. The chair creaked and wobbled when I sat down, alerting Grandma to my presence.

"How did you sleep last night, Sarah?" she asked while wiping her hands on her apron.

Last year, she had taught me how to cross-stitch and allowed me to sew the design that now decorated the waistband of the apron. The checks did not match the flowers on her faded cotton dress, but they made it easy to know where to place each stitch.

I knew she expected an answer, not like home where Momma yelled at us all the time to shut up.

Her eyes, now recessed and a lighter, almost translucent blue, twinkled as she donned a smile that brightened up the room. She walked over and gave me a hug adding the scent of Aqua Net and starch to the breakfast bouquet.

"Good. Lots better than at home. Someone is always making racket and Becky and Carla wiggle around too much. They kick me even when they're asleep." I pulled my legs up under the hem of my gown that she had made for me, attempting to fit the hem over my feet, but careful not to tear a hole in it. I didn't know when I'd get another one. Gowns, like days alone with Grandma, were prized possessions. The flannel warmed my toes and covered the bruises on the backs of my legs.

Grandma hummed "Amazing Grace" and flipped two eggs in the iron skillet that was still sizzling with bacon grease. The counter top remained dusted with flour and her favorite Vienna sausage can she always used to cut buttermilk biscuits. However, the biscuit I wanted would be tucked into the corner of the pan. She would have put it in last- the hard, lumpy one made from all the little pieces of dough left over after cutting.

A small, glass rooster and hen containing salt and pepper were placed in the center of the table. Next to them sat homemade watermelon rind preserves and a mason jar full of canned peaches. My mouth started to water.

Grandma had remembered these were my two favorite toppings for hot, buttered biscuits.

I was surprised to see that she had put the flowers I gave her into a jelly glass, which sat right smack dab in the middle of the table. In my ongoing attempt to make Momma happy, I sometimes picked her flowers from our yard. She usually threw them in the trash claiming they were just a bunch of nasty old weeds.

Grandma was pretty like the flowers. Momma called her a stupid, shriveled up old bag. I figured Momma must have bad eyes. Grandma never talked bad about Momma though. She was what people called "pretty on the inside" too. On the outside, she had tight curls framing pink cheeks, a warm body, and gentle hands.

Last night after putting my hair in pigtails, I watched as Grandma did her hair. She rolled strips of soft grey onto rollers and stuck a long, pink pin in them so they would stay on her head. She tied a headscarf over them; however, I bet the bristles still made her head hurt all night.

I felt so grownup when Grandma talked with me during breakfast. We kids weren't allowed to talk at the table because Momma said it got too loud plus it was rude to talk with food in our mouths.

The sun, shining through the window and framing four pictures of faded flowers on the vinyl tablecloth, announced it was time to get to work. I looked out of the open window, and a slight breeze ruffled the curtains. On the windowsill, Grandma had several little, hand-painted pots of cactus with tiny flowers of red or yellow blooming on them. We placed our dishes in the washtub by the sink and got dressed. It was a beautiful day for planting.

Grandma took my hand and we marched out to the shed where she kept her lawn and garden tools. She handed me the hoe with the shortest handle and took the other one for herself. Pancake shaped cactus had grown along her fence for as long as I can remember. Since last summer, they must have had babies or something because now some were growing right where Grandma always put her garden. Great. I wore tennis shoes, jeans, and a t-shirt and *everything* I was wearing had holes in them. This would be tricky.

We chopped along in silence for a good while. It felt nice working with her. I'd rather spend a whole day digging in the dirt and getting sunburned than stay at home. It was actually like a vacation compared to helping Momma take care of my brothers and sisters all day, plus doing chores.

Knowing my luck, today would have been clean-out-the-fridge day. Ugh! Gag! Butter bowls full of food that no longer resembled anything edible. I'd probably had to wash the dishes afterward, too. And even if I worked hard all day, Momma would find something wrong with it. Not that she ever needed much of a reason to punish us; especially me because I was the oldest and supposed to "be an example".

"Honey, are you alright? You look kind of sick." Grandma placed her fingers lightly on my forehead.

"Nah. I was thinking about what I'd be doing if I was at home. I don't know how you talked Momma into letting me come over today, but I'm glad you did. I wish I could come over more," Then quieter I muttered, "I wish I could live here."

Grandma didn't say anything. I glanced up, wondering if she had heard me. Grandma leaned on her hoe; her eyes looked all glassy and sad. *Oh, no. What did I do now? I'm always screwing things up.*

Wanting forgiveness, I asked, "Grandma, do you want me to hoe down the cactus? I don't mind. Really. I'll even chop down the ones along the fence, so maybe you won't have any to worry about next year."

"No. No, that's okay. We need...," suddenly her smile came back. "I like them. I want to keep them here because they remind me of something important." She chuckled at my confused expression. "Cactus are strong,

Sarah. They can live on little to nothing. Hard, dry dirt. Nothing but sun and an occasional sprinkle of rain. That little bit of rain has to be enough to last a long time. God doesn't love the cactus any less than the flowers; He just knows they can handle it."

She stopped for a minute and gave me a searching look. "Do you see how some of them have flowers on top? That is because they are so patient and good on the inside until one just pops out so everyone can see and admire its beauty. But it must have the sun to continue to grow and bloom. That is the key."

I raised my hand to shade my eyes and looked up at Grandma. I knew she was trying to explain something important to me so I remained quiet, trying to figure it out. In the awkward silence, I nudged the freshly turned dirt with my toe. The sun shimmered around her face and her dress swayed with the breeze. *I wonder if this is how angels look.*

"It is the same for us, Sarah. Some of us have a much harder life than others and it doesn't seem fair. But if we are patient, keep on doing the right thing, and trust in the Son..." she pointed up to the sky, "God's son, Jesus Christ, to always be there for us, then we will bloom. Hang in there, Sarah. It won't be easy, but He has promised us it will be worth it!"

*

In those days child abuse was a sick family secret forbidden to be mentioned by anyone to anyone. But that day, I knew she knew. I didn't get to visit her as often as I wanted, but she sprinkled some rain on me every chance she could. She would be the only person in my life who ever let me know, in her own way, that she understood. I might not have completely understood her story then, but like the cactus, it grew and bloomed within me through the years.

This is why today, on her casket, lay a dozen long-stemmed, red roses....and one tiny cactus.

I Dream of Horses!
By
Judith Victoria Douglas

I dream of horses!
They are massive in number,
All colors and sizes and types.
They're running, just running.

The sound of hammering hooves
Churning the fields into dust
Reverberates as a symphony
Of arrhythmic percussionists.

Terra thunder rumbling through
The mantle of the Earth
Announces they're coming,
As with the summer storm itself.

Each pounding hoof-strike
Batters the sod as they
Propel the undulating bodies
Over all manner of terrain.

Their chorus is without melody,
But pleasing all the same,
Each tone and volume
Accentuating the other.

Their aria proclaims their joy
In beating the wind,
Mastering their fleeting advance

'Tis the Season

As one with the herd.

Rapid breaths flutter soft nostrils
Regular as each hoof beat
Metronomes in quarter time
Measuring out their atonal song.

Anxious snorts punctuate
The myriad of sounds
As a kettledrum's occasional
Accentuating rumble.

It is power
And it is beauty,
It is chaos
And it is harmony.

It is horse.

I dream of horses!
They are massive in number,
All colors and sizes and types.
They're running, just running and
running and running.

From *Where the Horses Run, Book I, Mass Extinction. (as written by the main character, Elle)*

Bless It All Burt

By
Jeannie Faulkner Barber

Jolted from a delta sleep, Burt sat straight up—fists clenched, one eye squeezed tight, the other focused upward. *My God, what a horrendous noise.*

A pair of seagulls squawked, flapped their wings, and plummeted toward two red coral crabs.

The crustaceans scurried across the glossy shore to the shelter of a fractured rock.

"Thanks for the alarm clock, Mother Nature." Dirty nails scratched an abrasive nettle-like beard charting outlining his bony jaw. "What a glorious summer day." He sighed. Staunch, briny mist filled the air and left a salty paste on his tongue.

The sallow sun levitated above the horizon, and jagged shades of orange, red, and yellow rippled on the water like stadium pennants blown by the wind. Stiff from the sleeping on the pebbled ground, Burt struggled to stand on rubbery legs. An arch backwards brought a crisp pop like a muted firecracker. A rumble erupted from his stomach. The slow massage of the gaunt flesh eased the petition to eat.

Scattered around the small rocky alcove he called home, empty liquor bottles lay in a chorus of colors. The debris of containers emitted a pungent odor of alcohol—a sordid reminder that solid food was not his first priority.

His weathered hands brushed across the old blue jean shorts he wore, edges frayed and lifeless as a tatty mop head. Iridescent grains of parched sand tumbled downward. "Now where did I put my good shirt?" He grabbed the wrinkled garment, flopped on a soiled ball cap, and slipped into a pair of ratty sneakers.

Ruffled waves brushed the shore at the water's edge, and the cool, azure liquid filled Burt's palms. He patted his face. "Ah, time to start the daily routine."

Although a familiar figure in the seaport city of Chamberville, no one knew his story. For a few enigmatic cherished moments, Burton Daniel Davenport escaped to the past.

*

"Honey, don't forget we have dinner reservations at the Romulus tonight. The Windoms expect us...and on time. Don't be late again, there's a chance Senator Pettigrew might attend."

What a silly limelight charade we all continue to play. Burt tiptoed into the colorful decorated nursery, and Dena Davenport's instructions faded. The classic cheeriness in his wife's voice over the next scheduled social event irked him.

Little Starla slept in the pink and white, Casablanca crib. A mobile of fat cherubs overhead twirled to a melodious lullaby.

Across the room, the Swedish nanny slouched in the rocking chair, a book half open in her rotund lap. *No reason to be quiet, the woman snores like a bulldozer on nitrous.*

Tiny blonde ringlets framed an angelic face. He kissed Starla's forehead, grateful for her naïveté. The undeniable certainty his daughter would evolve to the same stagnant mind-set of her mother brought a wave of nausea. *Stay little, my princess. Avoid all of Mommy's stupid politics and mind games as long as you can.*

Dena mumbled something else, but to avoid a confrontation, Burt slipped out through the veranda to the five-car garage where a bevy of vehicles waited.

The manicured driveway of their palatial home stretched for a quarter of a mile before the electronic gate closed behind him. Tires gripped the asphalt, and after a quick right turn, the world whizzed past. Dreaded anticipation of the day's agenda lay ahead gripped his gut like a walk to the gallows. Congested traffic made the thirty-minute drive even more insufferable.

The sleek sports car screeched to a halt in his designated parking space. A sign in front of it read 'Reserved for CEO.' Burt hated his job, he hated his wife, and he hated his life.

"Good morning, Mr. Davenport." The latest receptionist put down a fingernail file and shot a quick smile.

Burt ignored the salutation and retreated through heavy ornate doors to his office. *So many new faces, it's easier not to remember any names. I doubt she'll last a whole week.*

A mountain of square, pastel pieces of paper, reminders of meetings, phone calls, and messages, plastered the top of a mahogany desk. Behind the closed door, a claustrophobic cloak engulfed him. "I feel as if I'm submerged in sand, my head above my own burial mound, encased like a corpse."

A panorama of the beach and waves allowed a momentary escape from the sense of suffocation until the abrupt intercom call forced back reality.

"Mr. Davenport?" The receptionist repeated, "It isn't good, Mr. Davenport. I'm so sorry."

What is this blonde moron of an employee saying?

Numerous phone calls followed, and soon the horror unfolded.

A plump, uniformed officer arrived and cautiously removed his hat to expose a baldhead. "Sir? Sir, are you okay? Do I need to call an ambulance?"

After another gurgle and gut-wrenching heave into the wastebasket, Burt looked up, tears flowing. "Dear God, tell me again what happened?"

The officer's eyes lowered. "Uh, yes sir, there was a

terrible fire, a gas line explosion in your neighborhood. So far, we have not found any survivors. We presume your family and home perished. Everything for several blocks is gone. My sincere condolences."

*

Burt pulled the sweat-stained cap down over his shaggy gray hair and gripped a rusty handle of the old lawnmower. Calloused, tan hands coaxed the old piece of machinery forward. On weak, arthritic knees, he padded across the silvery silt. Reminiscent of a snail's route, a patterned track followed behind. He knew it must look odd, even somewhat comical…a grown man forcing a lawnmower across the beach. Thoughts turned to the constant harassment endured from on-lookers. Spring break visitors were the worst, bellowing crude obscenities accompanied by haunting laughter. Undeterred, and with a wave of a hand, he returned their banter with the comment, "Bless it all."

In need of the bitter fuel his body demanded, he mowed lawns for any amount of money. Summertime offered the most lucrative opportunities for this meager livelihood. However, many of the townsfolk refused to contribute to such a vile cause. Even so, he would bid them a 'bless it all,' ignore the scorn in their eyes, and walk away.

The lawnmower not only provided a means to afford the demon-filled addiction, but also his only friendship. He worked meticulously on the rickety contraption. "Yeah, we're both worn out, but I believe we can make it one more season."

One humid July afternoon, remnants of sand gnashing in the wheels, Burt pushed the aged machine across a busy intersection. Horns blared as he lumbered through the walkway and forced it upon the curb at the corner of Royal and Crestview. Covered in sweat, he placed the mower near the entrance of Charlie O's Bar. "You wait here."

A string of bells jingled as the door opened to reveal

cool air-conditioned surroundings.

"Hi there," a small voice said.

"Who are you?" Burt's gruff voice rattled.

"I'm Polly. My uncle Charlie let me help him today. He's in the back right now. Who are you?" Golden corkscrew curls outlined the young girl's face.

Burt blinked hard and grabbed his chest, propelled back to the day in the nursery. *Starla? No, you can't be...I left her in the crib.* White-knuckles clutched the counter.

"Are you okay, mister? I can get help if you're sick or something." Polly reached out, but he recoiled at the approach.

"Don't be so nosy. Besides, you can't help me."

"I bet I can. I'm eight years old, you know." She stood with hands planted on her hips.

"Look, I need to talk to your Uncle Charlie. I have to make a...a purchase, one of those pretty green bottles over there."

Polly struggled with chubby legs to climb upon a stool behind the bar. "Which one?"

"Better go get your uncle. I don't want you to drop it."

"I won't. Which one?"

A shaking finger pointed to the selection.

The glass door slid back, and Polly retrieved a container of cheap wine. It thudded on the wooden counter. "That will be six dollars, mister."

"How the hell, I mean, how do you know how much it costs?" A frown furrowed his brow.

"I told you, I'm eight years old. I'll be in third grade when school starts. Anyway, that's what the red sticker says." A crescent smile appeared.

He rammed a hand into the ragged shorts pocket, and a finger plunged through the thin material. "What? Where's my wadded ten spot?"

"Don't you have any money?"

"I did, but there's a damn hole here."

"It isn't nice to curse. My Aunt Sally tells Uncle Charlie not to all the time. Hey, I can pay for it." The little girl unzipped a pink, plastic purse, reached inside, and thrust a closed fist.

"Forget it, kid."

"Aunt Sally says the Bible tells us we're supposed to share. Please, let me give this to you. I know Uncle Charlie don't want you to be thirsty. Besides, this is supposed to bring good luck. Maybe you'll find the money you lost." Small fingers uncurled one at a time to reveal the treasure. An open palm cradled a smooth sand dollar.

"Well, bless it all," he replied.

*

"Mr. Davenport, are you going to work late tonight?" the nasal voice of the receptionist blared over the intercom.

"Huh? What? No." Burt rubbed his forehead. The shiny Rolex felt heavy on his wrist. It was after six o'clock. *What happened to me? Did I doze off?* His belly growled in anticipation of food. The jacket to a navy Armani suit hung on the back of the leather executive chair. He slipped it on, straightened his tie, and reached in the pants pocket for some car keys. "What the hell is this?" A few grains of sand and a sand dollar tumbled onto the glossy desk. Breathless, he slumped into the chair, heart pounding, and mouth cotton-dry. Pictures of Dena and Starla covered the credenza. Mouth agape, tears streamed down his cheeks and left a salty taste on his tongue.

*

An explosion of lightning serrated the sky. Cool pellets of rain fell hard and fast. Burt gasped for breath, shook his head to erase the images of the dream, and grabbed a thin ragged blanket. Bolts of neon guided a pathway to his friend. Sobs came in spurts while he patted the rusty, old lawnmower. "Bless it all," he whispered.

Nathaniel and Caroline
By
Ann Everett

The first time I saw Nathaniel, he was standing ankle-deep in the stream running through Hudnall Olson's property. I always took a shortcut across the Olson place to go to my grandma's house, and often waded in the cool water to get some relief from the scorching summer heat.

He wasn't wearing a shirt and his jeans rode low enough, skin that hadn't seen the light of day formed a pale ring around his waist. The rest of his body was the color of honey. Golden honey.

From a small thicket of wild plum trees, I watched him cup his hands, fill them with water, and splash his face and neck, the overflow trickling down his body. He had Jesus hair. Long, flowing, curly, Jesus hair.

He was the most beautiful man I'd ever seen.

"You might as well come out, whoever you are. I know you're there. I can even hear you breathing from here," he said into empty space.

The remark caught me off-guard because I didn't think I'd been breathing at all. At the sight of him, my lungs seized up and my heart started to pound. Partly from the surprise of seeing a stranger in the woods, but mostly because of his appearance.

I swallowed hard and called my emotions to order. I couldn't show any fear. My daddy had taught me animals could sense fear and I figured that carried over to the human animal as well. I stepped into the clearing and he turned to face me.

Standing half-naked before me, droplets of water

clung to his lean body, sunlight reflecting off them like morning dew. A wide smile spread across his unshaven face. His blue eyes gleamed like a coyote that'd just happened upon a nest of baby ducks.

"Well, well, Girly-Girl. What are you doing out here all by yourself?" he asked, leaning over and picking up his shirt.

"I'm on the way home from my grandma's house. I always walk this way," I said, with some authority in my voice. "You're not Jesus, are you?"

He broke into a full laugh, causing his honey-colored mane to fly wildly about his face. "No, I'm not Jesus. I'm about as far from Jesus as you can get."

Without thinking, I took a step back.

He must have sensed my concern, because he lifted his hands, palms out, in front of his chest, as if surrendering. "Whoa. I didn't mean to scare you," he said, his smile disappearing.

I straightened my shoulders. "You didn't scare me."

His smile returned. "Nothing wrong with being scared. Fear can keep you safe, help you make the right decisions. Fear's a good thing. Especially for little girly-girls like you. There are a lot of big bad wolves in the world waiting for *Little Red Riding Hood* on her way to grandma's house."

"Why do you keep calling me Girly-Girl?"

He put his shirt on, but didn't button it. "Because you *are* a girly-girl. Look at you with your ruffled blouse, big brown eyes, and that pretty red hair all tied up with a pink bow. You're definitely a girly-girl. I bet you're a daddy's girl."

"I am not," I declared, pretending to be insulted. But the truth was I loved the way the words "girly-girl" rolled off his tongue.

He stepped forward and extended his hand. "I'm Nathaniel Tate."

I took another step back.

He withdrew his hand and smiled. "I see. We need to know each other better before we shake hands. Right?"

Unable to help myself, I started to laugh. "Wait a minute. Your name is Nate Tate? What happened? Didn't your momma like you?"

He twisted his mouth around, fought a smile, but lost. "My momma likes me just fine. It's a family name. Besides, I don't go by Nate. I go by Nathaniel, so most of the time people don't make the rhyming connection. But, you're a sharp little tack, aren't you?"

Finally feeling at ease, I stuck out my hand. "Well, nice to meet you, Nate Tate. I'm Caroline Adams."

His hand was cool from the stream. Mine was warm either from the August heat or his touch. I wasn't sure.

He smiled down at me. "Hmmm, the name suits you. So, I guess you've decided I'm not dangerous?"

I pulled my hand away. "Are you dangerous?"

"I can be," he said, keeping his smile in place. "In ways you're too young to know about. How old are you? Fourteen?"

"I have you know, I'm sixteen. And a half," I said, insulted by the question. "How old are you?"

"Old enough to know your daddy wouldn't like you being out here in the woods with me."

I walked over and leaned against a big oak tree, its leaves rustling from a sudden breeze. He turned, followed me, sat down by the stream, and stuck his feet back in.

I took my shoes off, waded into the water, and gracefully moved through it as if it were my dance partner. "I've never seen you before. This place belongs to Mr. Olson and he doesn't like people coming on his property. If he finds out, you'll get in trouble."

"I have permission to be here," he said.

"Really? You know Mr. Olson?"

"He's my uncle."

"Nuh-uh. I've known him all my life and he's never mentioned any relatives. So, who are you?"

He puckered his lips, and then the pucker turned into a grin. "So, you've known my uncle for sixteen years. And a half."

"Nobody likes a smarty-pants," I said, crossing my arms.

"I am his nephew and the reason you've never heard of me is because until recently, he and my mother didn't speak. They had a falling out a long time ago. Actually, over this land. But now, he's old and sick and they decided to kiss and make-up. When he's gone, this property will be mine and then little Girly-Girl; you'll have to get *my* permission to walk across this place to your grandma's house."

"So, you're gonna be my neighbor," I said, unable to hide my excitement.

"Not for a while. I've got to finish school first. I've got one more year."

"You'll graduate high school next year?" I stopped pacing and stood directly in front of him.

"No. I'll finish *college,* next year."

"Oh, college," I said slowly, trying to let the word sink in. I walked out of the water, sat down and put my shoes on. "It was nice to meet you, Nate Tate." I turned to go, but he called after me.

"Hey, Girly-Girl. Will I see you again?"

My heart stopped. I turned to look at him. "I don't know. You're in college and that makes you dangerous after all."

"You're the dangerous one, Girly-Girl. But in a year, when I come back, you'll be seventeen. And a half. Then you won't be quite so dangerous."

*

For the next two years, while the big oak effortlessly marked time, I thought about Nathaniel Tate and wondered if I would see him again. From time to time, until the weather made it unbearable, I went to the stream and dangled my feet in the water and remembered how he looked on that hot August day in nineteen sixty-five.

I was lying on a quilt under the oak tree, staring up at a cloudless sky, through branches about to burst forth with leaves.

"Well, well, Girly-Girl. Look at you. All grown up," he said from behind me.

Startled, I sat up and smiled at him, my heart pounded so hard I was sure he could hear it. "Hello, Nate Tate," I said, trying to sound offhand.

He walked over, sat down next to me, put his finger under my chin and lifted my face to his. Then he kissed me.

*

As if on cue, Rachel, our eight-year-old daughter sighed. "I love that part, Momma."

Fighting tears, my bottom lip quivered. "I know you do."

"I do, too," Nate said from the doorway.

Jumping from her seat, Rachel ran and hugged him. "Daddy, you tell me your version."

He sat down next to me and Rachel wedged herself between us.

"Well, August in Texas is like the waiting room to Hell. Grass turns brown and the earth beneath cracks open. Even the mighty oak's leaves wither and curl as the sun hammers down, with no mercy for plant, animal, or man."

"Under normal circumstances, I wouldn't choose to spend my vacation here, but this wasn't a typical situation. My only living uncle on my mother's side was dying and he had summoned Mom and me to come to Texas."

"I'd never met Uncle Hudnall, because he and Mom had a falling out before I was born. But when you're old and sick, family becomes more important."

As he said those words, from the corner of my eye, I saw him look at me. He held his gaze for a long moment and when I didn't acknowledge him, he continued.

"Uncle Hudnall's time was almost up and he'd drawn

up a will leaving everything to me. He'd never married, so Mom and I were the only family he had. I was only twenty-one and when I found out I'd be a land owner, I was overwhelmed."

"At the time, I lived in Fullerton, California and attended California State University. We lived only fifteen miles from the beach. I planned to sell the place as soon as Uncle Hudnall was gone, and go back to Fullerton."

"I'd spent most of that morning walking the property. I'd calculated how much the acreage would bring and determined I'd be able to pay off school loans, buy a new car, and have a little nest egg left over."

"I had my future all planned out. But then, I met your mother and she changed everything. Now, you go outside and play. I need to talk to your momma. When I'm done, we'll walk down to the stream."

Rachel trotted out the door, her red curls bounced in rhythm with her steps. Nate cleared his throat and I turned my attention back to him. He pulled a coin from his pocket and held it up. "Do you know what this is?" he asked.

"Yes, congratulations."

He rubbed it between his fingers. "Two years, Caroline. Two years sober. Two years living in this house together but separate and all you can say is congratulations?"

I turned to face him, but diverted my eyes. "What do you want me to say?"

"I guess I don't want you to say anything. I miss you. I miss holding you. I miss hearing the rhythm of your breathing at night. I don't want to be punished anymore."

I looked up at him with fire in my eyes. "This is not about punishment. It's about survival. *My* survival. James was our son, not just yours. His death was an accident. It wasn't your fault. You don't get to choose who lives or dies. But you do get to choose to go on living or crawl into a bottle."

"Caroline," he said, reaching for me.

I pulled away. "The day James died, you died too and I've had to mourn you both. I'm worn out, Nate. I can't do this anymore."

"You don't have to. It's different this time."

He took my hand. "What makes it different?" I asked.

"I don't know. I just know it is." He carried my hand to his lips and kissed it. "This time, I need *you* more than I need a drink."

For the first time in two years, I looked at him, *really* looked at him. There was determination in his eyes. Something I'd not seen in a long time.

The door swung open. Rachel ran in and shouted. "C'mon Daddy, let's go."

He stood up, and pulled me up with him. "Come to the stream with us."

"Yeah, come with us, Momma," Rachel begged. "You never come with us."

I shook my head. "I don't know."

Nate took advantage of the situation. He hugged me to him, knowing I wouldn't pull away in front of Rachel. "Come with us, please," he whispered into my hair.

"What is it with you and the stream? It's just water," I said, loving the way his arms felt around me.

"Oh, that's where you're wrong, Girly-Girl. It's magical. It's where we began. Where we shared our first kiss. Where we fell in love. Where I proposed."

Rachel's eyes begged for more detail.

"You know what the five senses are?" Nate asked her.

Rachel shook her head.

"They're sound, sight, touch, smell and taste and every time we go to the stream the magic floods those senses. When we were young, and the first cold snap came, your momma and I would take a quilt and a sleeping bag and spend the night under the old oak tree."

My heart and eyes softened at the memory.

"We'd spread out the quilt; put our sleeping bag on top and zip ourselves in. I'd pull your momma close and let the stream work its magic. Do you remember, Caroline?"

I closed my eyes. "Of course, I do."

He hugged me tighter against him. "First, our hearing would overflow with the sound of rushing water. As people built their first fire of the season, the scent of burning wood wafted the air and filled our sense of smell. Next, we'd be awestruck, watching the stars appear in the night sky. I'd hold your momma so close, I could feel her heart beating against mine."

"That's only four, Daddy," Rachel said. "You left one out. You have the water for sound, the firewood for smell, the stars for sight and momma's heartbeat for touch. You left out taste. What did you taste?"

He lifted my face to his and kissed me. "I tasted love. When I kiss your momma, she tastes like love."

The Right Call
By
Vivra P. Beene

"Heather, just shut up about my love life!" said Laurie. "I don't have time for one. When I'm not waitressing, I'm chauffeuring a ten-year old. Seems I'm always on the road—to work, to ball practice, to these games."

Leaning forward in the lawn chair, she gripped its arms with white knuckles. Her son Toby was at bat, his team needed runs, and she held her breath.

Heather let out an exasperated sigh. "It's been two years since Jeff died. Toby needs a father-figure, especially when he's so interested in sports."

"And where am I supposed to meet eligible father-figures?"

"Ball games?" Heather suggested.

"Ha! Look around. The father-figures all have wife-figures with them. There's not one single male parent here." Toby hit the ball; the umpire called foul.

Heather thumped the chair arm. "Dang, this game is frustrating," she spat.

"Why? We're winning. Way to go, babe," she yelled as Toby connected and made it to first base.

"Because I can't get mad at the umpire," said Heather.

"He is kind of cute isn't he?"

Heather looked sideways at her friend. "That's not the reason. You know I get my kicks heckling umps about bad calls, but this guy is good—hasn't made a call I've disagreed with yet."

Toby stole third, and Laurie cheered again. She watched the home plate umpire. He was quite attractive, black shorts and gray uniform shirt taut on his muscled body. She wondered if his face, obscured by the regulation mask, looked as good as the rest of him, and what color hair was the black baseball cap hiding?

Two more runs, top of the sixth, Toby's team was ahead seven to five. As if he'd read Laurie's mind, the umpire strolled to the fence, throwing down his mask and cap and wiping his forehead with the back of his arm. Smiling broadly, he looked right at her. Jet-black hair framed navy-blue eyes in a tanned, rugged face. Motioning to her, he unstrapped his watch and held it out. "Would you mind holding this until the end of the game?"

Laurie smiled and with a shaking hand took the watch. "Nice calling, Ump," she replied.

"I appreciate that. Most parents just complain, very few praise. Thanks."

"You're welcome," she said. Heather looked suitably ashamed.

It was a close game, Toby's team lost by one run. Parents folded chairs, rounded up offspring, and headed for the parking lot. Toby left with teammates to eat pizza and autopsy the game.

Heather juggled chairs and jangled car keys. "I'll go on to the car and wait for you," she said. "So you two can get acquainted. Tell him I left because I don't like an umpire I can't gripe at."

"I'm only waiting to give him his watch back," Laurie protested. "He's not interested in me. Besides, I bet he's married with six kids."

"Don't tell me he's not interested. I saw the way he watched you. Every time you went to the concession stand, he was on pins until you came back. And he's not wearing a ring."

"So?" Laurie retorted.

"Here he comes," said Heather. She waved a salute.

"Don't be too long," she called over her shoulder. "I'm ready to eat."

"Thanks for keeping my watch." The umpire walked over to Laurie. "Which one was your son?"

"Toby Landers," she answered. "I'm Laurie." They strolled to the gate.

"I'm Jim McDonald. You've got a good team there. They were ahead until that error in the final inning. You like baseball?"

"Love it," she replied. "I'm a sports nut. We're looking forward to football after this."

"I hear you. I love to umpire. My ex-wife hated sports. That, among other things, was what ruined our marriage." Jim took her left hand. "Is there a man in your life, Laurie Landers?"

Their eyes met, and for a moment she was too breathless to answer him. "Just Toby," she said finally. "Toby's dad was killed two years ago. Car wreck. Drunk driver." She shuddered.

"I'm sorry, I didn't mean to upset you," Jim said, and then more cheerfully, "Listen, I'm umpiring a game in Tyler on Friday. Come and watch it? We'll eat afterwards. Please?"

To her surprise, she agreed.

"Great! Game starts at six. I'll be watching for you."

On Friday, with pounding heart, Laurie drove to Tyler. She'd wanted to back out, using the excuse that Toby had ball practice. "And besides, I don't know where the ball park is…"

"I'll take Toby to practice," insisted Heather. "And the ball park is easy to find." She drew a map. "Turn right on Fairfax, left on Turner. You can't miss Turner, there's a fire station on the corner. The ballpark is about two miles on the right. Now, go. Have fun."

Right on Fairfax, and the fire station was obvious. A fire truck, lights flashing, sirens wailing, was pulling out. Traffic was at a standstill.

"What am I getting myself into?" she pondered, waiting patiently for the vehicle to move away. "I don't know this guy, and I'm driving all this way to watch a game when I don't know a single kid on either team. I'm going to sit there looking dumb just to watch an umpire. I should turn around and go home."

Sirens were still echoing when she arrived at the ballpark. She scanned the field for Jim, but didn't see him.

Dare she ask at the scorekeeper's table if Jim had arrived? Had she come to the wrong ballpark? Maybe the game he was umpiring was across town...out of town...somewhere else.

Snippets of conversation drifted to her.

"...the ump hasn't arrived..."

"...he's been late before. He'll be here..."

"...when Jim gets here, send him right out..."

Where was he? The game started with a substitute umpire. Laurie watched the first innings, and then decided to leave. Turning to go, she collided with a breathless youngster.

"Sorry," he gasped. "Where's the scorekeeper?"

Laurie pointed.

"Thanks. I've got to let her know there's been a wreck. The umpire won't be here."

"Do you mean Jim McDonald? What happened? Is he okay?"

"Don't know, ma'am. He's alive—they don't know what injuries..."

"Hospital?" Laurie interrupted.

"St. Michael's."

Laurie shouted thanks as she ran to her car.

The emergency room waiting area at St. Michael's was crowded. Laurie cornered one of the busy nurses and asked about Jim.

"His hip is broken. The doctor's with him. If you sit in the waiting room, we'll call you." She walked brusquely away.

Laurie sank onto a vinyl bench and studied the people around her. She heard Jim's name mentioned by an elderly couple and younger woman huddled in one corner. Suddenly, Laurie felt out of place. What was she doing here? She didn't know Jim. She hadn't given any thought to others that might know him better, his family and friends. A girlfriend? Those people must be his mom and dad. And the woman?

The woman was blond, stunning in a purple figure-hugging dress. She paced, biting fingernails.

A nurse called. "McDonald family? You can go in and see him now. Family only," she added.

Laurie fidgeted. She watched the family leave, then after a minute found the nurse and asked, "Would it be possible for me to speak to Jim McDonald, too?"

"Are you related?"

"No, I…"

"Sorry, family only. They're getting him ready for x-rays. His mom, dad, and wife are with him now."

"Wife?" Laurie echoed.

"Mrs. McDonald. That's the name she gave." The nurse scurried off, following a doctor into the interior of the hospital.

With feet of lead, Laurie walked outside. The ambulance driver was smoking a cigarette. She stopped and asked about the wreck.

"Wasn't his fault, Miss. He had nowhere to go. Drunken fool pulled right out in front of him. Needed 'Jaws' to cut him out. Had to work fast, gasoline was leaking. If there'd been a fire, he wouldn't have made it." He shook his head. "The time it took the fire truck to get there, it would have been all over. The drunk wasn't even hurt. Walked away. Guess the Good Lord looks after kids and fools—even drunk fools."

In a daze, Laurie drove home, not knowing whom she hated most, drunk drivers or men who told lies.

Three days later, there was a message on her

answering machine. "Hey girl, wish you'd come and see me. I won't be able to umpire any more this season. I need someone to talk baseball with. The nurse told me you came to the hospital when they brought me in, so you know where I am. Room 432. Call me. Please?"

"The nerve of the guy," she told Heather. "I'm not going to call him. Shoot, his wife might answer!"

Toby, who didn't know all the details, thought Jim was wonderful. "He said I had a terrific throwing arm, and he's going to give me some pointers."

"Well, I don't know when, kid," Laurie responded. "I don't imagine we'll be seeing any more of him."

"Aw, Mom, you never date anybody I like. Jim's cool."

She ruffled his shaggy hair. "Too cool for me, partner."

Jim left more messages. He was out of the hospital. He wanted to talk to her. He left his number.

Curious to know how he was getting along, but remembering the attractive Mrs. McDonald, Laurie refused to let her curiosity get the better of her. With a wife as attractive as that, Jim was a heel for thinking about another woman.

It was a Monday, three weeks and umpteen messages after the hospital released Jim, that she had a visitor. Curiously, she watched as a red Pontiac Grand Am turned into her driveway. Her heart froze when she recognized the driver. Mrs. McDonald. Hmm, was she coming to warn her away from her man?

She braced herself to answer the doorbell.

"Mizz Landers?" The woman's voice was smooth as honey.

Laurie took a deep breath. "Yes, and you're Mrs. McDonald. Look, I want you to know that I have no designs on your husband. I'm not going to come between you; I'm not that kind of person."

The woman's mouth dropped open. "My husband?

But you don't know my…" Her head went back, and she started to laugh. "Oh honey, you think Jim's my husband?"

"You're Mrs. McDonald, and you're definitely not old enough to be his mother," Laurie retorted.

"Yes, I'm Mrs. McDonald—Jim's sister-in-law. I'm married to his brother, John." She laughed. "Jim's been divorced for over two years now. His ex-wife is in Florida, married with two kids."

Tears prickled Laurie's eyes.

Mrs. McDonald explained. "Jim sent me to find out why you hadn't called him. He's really fallen for you. Won't you come and see him? He's at his parent's house, so you'll be suitably chaperoned, unfortunately—they can be a drag. He'll be with them until he's able to get around better, then he'll go back to his own apartment."

Laurie couldn't stop the grin. "Mrs. McDonald, thank you for coming to explain everything. I really thought Jim was lying to me. I'm so glad he wasn't."

"Honey, Jim couldn't lie his way out of a paper sack." She hugged Laurie. "Please call me Anne. Say you'll visit him? It would do him so much good. Oh, he said he'd like to see your son, as well. Toby, isn't it?"

Before she left, Anne made Laurie promise to think about visiting Jim.

It didn't take her long to think.

The next afternoon, she sat with Jim in his parent's back yard, sipping iced tea and watching Toby pitch to Jim's father.

Jim held her hand and looked into her eyes. "Yep," he said, nodding seriously. "When I called Anne and asked her to visit you to find out why you hadn't answered my messages—you know what?"

"Tell me."

"It was definitely the right call."

Seasons of Change
By
Elizabeth Baker

The boy stood perfectly still. The smells were new, but at the same time vaguely familiar: Summer sun and grass ripening in the heat. Maybe he had been here before. Maybe he stood on this exact spot. Grandpa said he had. Not long after he arrived in this place Grandpa told him the story of coming here with his mom when he was five-years-old. Now, he was ten, and five was half a lifetime away.

He dropped down in the grass and rolled to his back studying the clouds as the fading sun added pink to the whites and blues. He rolled to his stomach, propped himself on his elbows and looked at the meadow from this new angle. Two mysteries had been puzzling him all week. The first was why Grandpa's farm was not a real farm, and the second was why his mom sent him here alone.

Grandpa said it had once been a real farm with cows and tractors and even a pig, but now, there was a big mall just down the road, and when the boy climbed the tallest tree he could see all the new houses with their new fences and little new trees just beyond the meadow. He wondered what the children in those houses thought as they looked out high windows or peeked through the boards of their fences at this place of grass and tall trees. To Brian, all this looked and smelled like a farm.

Over by the back fence there was a creek, and the meadow was so large he grew tired when he tried to run all the way around the edge twice without stopping. Perhaps it had been a real farm when his mom was a little girl.

That brought him to the second mystery. Boarding the plane without Mom had been scary; a fact that he would never have admitted to the guys back in San Diego. Why had she made him go alone? She said Grandpa only sent money for one ticket and besides, she had to stay home and pack so they could join Daddy at his new assignment. He doubted that was the whole truth. His family had moved before. When your Dad's in the Navy that's just how it is.

Suddenly, something moved not far away and any thoughts of mystery were quickly swallowed up by a new curiosity.

At the edge of the meadow an old cabin had fallen to ruin. Nothing was supposed to live there, but while the boy watched a mother skunk crept from under the pile of rubble. After a hesitant look around, she signaled and four baby skunks walked into the evening light. He wanted to run and pick them up like kittens, but even a city kid knows you can't do that. Still, it couldn't hurt to sneak closer and watch where they were going.

*

On the opposite side of the meadow, an old man in coveralls shaded his eyes. The grass was thin and it didn't take long to locate his grandson creeping along on all fours. Was that boy playing Cowboys and Indians all by himself? Then he saw the object of the boy's curiosity.

The old man's mind gave his body a command to move quickly, but a sudden pain in his back and chest gave a different command. He caught his breath, straightened and slowed to a stop. "Brian," he called, hoping his voice was loud enough for the boy to hear but not so loud it startled Mrs. Skunk.

His grandson looked up and grinned pointing to the slowly retreating skunk. Grandpa nodded and smiled, then motioned for Brian to leave the skunk alone and come to him. Reluctantly the boy did as he was told.

"Did you see 'em, Grandpa? Weren't they

somethin'!"

"I saw them, Brian." The light in the eyes of his only grandchild was sweet elixir to his soul. He hardly noticed the continuing pain. "Why, did you know when I was a boy that skunk's great-great-great grandma was raising a passel o' kits in that same spot?"

"Really?"

"Really. But, we need to go back to the house. Your Grandma has supper almost ready."

They walked a few yards in silence then the boy spoke. "Grandpa, when I grow up will the skunks still be there?"

They had reached a rise in the meadow and the old man could see how the land around him had changed. There was a time he thought he could hold his own against the steady march of the city. Then came financial realities. And, last month the final reality of the doctor's prognosis fell with a blow. Change was part of life.

"No, son," he answered honestly. "One day soon, there won't be a meadow. Or, a barn. Or, a creek."

Brian was quiet. He had not been raised here. He had seldom even visited here. But, it was sad to think of the farm and the skunks going away and his grandson never experiencing all this again. His grandson's wrinkled young brow betrayed emotions he didn't have words to express.

"It's okay," Grandpa assured him and tousled the boy's hair with a gnarled, weathered hand. "God never intended things on this earth to stay forever." The boy looked at him with doubtful eyes. "Don't worry. I suspect Mrs. Skunk will find a new house. Maybe she'll join her kinfolk down by Wilson Pond."

That seemed to comfort him. The boy's step was a little lighter as he walked ahead of the slow, old man. Then Brian stopped and turned. "Where will you and Grandma live?"

His Grandpa looked at him for a long moment then spoke slowly. "Brian, there's something I want to tell you.

Something important." The boy gave him his full attention and Grandpa had to clear his throat. "God put us in a world of change. We can't get away from it. But, we must never forget that even though things about us change, God never does. He was faithful before the change came along and He will be faithful after. We may not want things to change, but if we keep watching, we will find that God makes a new way for us to be happy."

"I'll remember, Grandpa," the boy spoke clearly and nodded, but he did not turn around. He stood in the gathering dusk and looked directly at the man as though reminding him that he had still not answered his question. The skunk might find a hole along the bank of Wilson Pond, but what about his grandparents?

Grandpa smiled. He liked the boy's directness and grit. "I guess you still want to know about Grandma and me?" Brian nodded. "Well, I can't rightly say. Mrs. Skunk can find a new house, but people need more than a house with walls and floors. People need a home."

Brian waited silently.

"Son, a home is a place where you know you belong and you know you will always be welcome. Grandma and I have made a home together for a long, long time. But, it looks like soon we will find homes in separate places. Your Grandma will most likely share a home with your Uncle Kenny and his wife, Sharon." He paused. "As for me, well, I am looking forward to moving to a different place. It will be a home that doesn't change. A place where I belong. A place where Jesus went long ago and is waitin' for me."

Neither of them moved for a long moment then Grandpa started along the path and Brian fell in step beside him. He wondered how much the young boy understood of what he was trying to say. He had asked Brian's mother if he could personally tell his only grandchild of his impending death, but he had never imagined how difficult it would be. Maybe the boy was just too young or didn't understand that his grandpa was talking about heaven.

"Grandpa?" the voice was soft but steady.

"Yes, son."

"You remember what you said about change being okay, 'cause God makes a new way to be happy?"

"Yes."

"I wish things could just stay like they were in the first place."

He nodded. "At times I do, too."

"But, if you and the farm and the skunk has got to change, I sure am glad God made a place for you where things don't change no more."

"Me, too, Brian. Me, too."

The kitchen light came on and a golden glow spilled through the window. Grandpa swung open the yard gate and then paused. "I just thought of one more thing I hope you remember."

"Nobody can stop things changin', but as the moments pass by, don't forget to enjoy 'em if you can. You may not be able to hold on to 'em forever, but you can touch them as they pass and be happy because the good times came."

"We got a lot we need to talk about. And we will. But right now, I think I smell Grandma's fried chicken. That big ol' platter's probably piled high with golden brown pieces that are juicy on the inside and crispy on the out. Let's go change it to a platter of crumbs."

Summer
By
Jean Lauzier

Those lazy days of summer,
With hammocks in the shade.
Bare feet on the cool grass,
   I've really got it made.

There's burgers on the grill,
Watermelon cold and sweet.
Homemade vanilla ice cream,
   It's really quite a treat.

The smell of honeysuckle,
Sun shining down so bright.
A gentle breeze is blowing,
Slowly day turns into night.

A million stars twinkle above me,
As fireflies dance in the wind.
The crickets sing to each other,
Wish summer would never end.

Summertime
By
Janice Ernest

It was the last day of school for the fourth grade. Shawn squirmed in her desk chair. *I wish the bell would hurry up and ring.* Her whole body felt restless, fidgety.

The intercom clicked to life and the principal, Mrs. Vickery, cleared her throat.

"Children, the bell is about to ring. I just want to wish you all a good summer vacation and I will see you next year." The loud speaker clicked off and a low 'bong' signaled the end of the school day.

Shawn jumped up from her desk, grabbed her books, and made a beeline for the door. Summer had begun and she didn't want to miss even one moment of it. She raced to get onto Bus Number Three and away the bus went on its final journey of the year.

Upon arriving home, she leapt off the bus, turned and told the bus-driver goodbye, and then raced into the house. Her mom was still at work at the hospital, so she fixed herself a snack of two chocolate chip cookies and a glass of milk, scarfed them down, and then raced outside to enjoy the summer.

Blackie, her small, mixed-breed, shorthaired, pudgy dog was already enjoying basking in the early summertime sun. He smiled a doggy grin at her, mouth open and tongue hanging out to one side. Upon hearing her arrival, he immediately began the process of trying to roll his rather round body over so that he might greet her. With great effort after two or three tries, he managed to come topside up, jump to his short legs, and race to greet her with licks and pounces.

"Oh, Blackie, it's summer, it's summer!" she said as she grabbed his front paws and did a dance with him.

*

All Blackie got out of this conversation was "…blah, Blackie, blah, blah, blah, blah, blah blah!" He knew, though, that whatever Shawn was saying it was good because of the inflection in her voice. Also, she only danced with him on grand occasions.

Maybe I am going to get a snack or a pat or a toy or a… His doggy thoughts roamed on and on until she released him and he brought his front paws back down to the porch.

*

For the next two years, this pattern for the last day of school continued. In seventh grade, Shawn met what she thought was the forever love of her life. His name was Jeremy Strickland and he was an eighth grader. She didn't know what it was about him, maybe his thick blond hair, or his funny sense of humor, or the freckles over his nose, but he was the bomb. As the school year progressed, they could be seen holding hands, walking down the hall together. They were inseparable.

As the school year came to an end, he asked her to go steady with him. She accepted. Theirs was a love made in heaven. There was only one problem. His family was going to be gone from June through August and they would not be able to see one another. They swore to text and to stay in touch.

The last day of school came and Shawn didn't even flinch while sitting in her chair. She longed for the year to continue so that she and Jeremy might see one another. Inevitably, the intercom clicked on and the principal repeated her yearly speech, then the bell, like a harbinger of doom, rang. Shawn gathered her things together and walked to get on the bus like a prisoner being led to execution. *How will I survive summer without Jeremy?*

She climbed slowly off the bus, didn't even stop to wish the driver a happy summer, just slunk up the sidewalk and into the house. She didn't want cookies and milk. She dropped her books, walked through the house, and out into the back yard. Blackie, now too old to roll onto his back in the sun, lay on his stomach on a soft rug in the sunlight. He opened his eyes and looked up at Shawn.

"Hi, Blackie, it's summer." She sighed.

His response was to wag his tail once then resettle into his nap.

She sat on the back porch step with her hands in her lap, contemplating the lonely months ahead of her, when the phone rang. "Alright, already, I'm coming," she spoke to the air as she slowly got up, went in the house, and picked up the receiver.

"Hey, Shawn, it's Maggie, what are you doing tomorrow? Mom and Dad are taking us to the lake. Would you like to go?"

"No, I'll just stay here, but thanks for the offer."

"Are you sure? We're going to have watermelon and homemade ice cream and go tubing, maybe even ride the Jet Ski. Come on and go with us. It won't be the same without you."

"I'll have to ask my mom. Let me call you back."

*

That evening when Shawn's mom arrived home, Shawn had cooked Hamburger Helper Lasagna and made a salad for the two of them. She also noticed that Shawn had done some laundry and her bedroom looked clean. "Okay, young lady, what are you wanting from me?"

"Just to let you know I love you and to ask if I can go with Maggie and her parents to the lake tomorrow."

"Well, let's see, your room looked clean when I got home. The laundry is done. I suppose you can go."

Shawn called Maggie, "Hey, Maggie, Mom said I could go, but I don't plan on having fun. Jeremy is out of town."

"Oh, stop worrying about Jeremy, you and I will have lots of fun. I can't wait. We'll pick you up at about eight tomorrow morning."

At eight sharp, Maggie and her parents pulled up the drive in their SUV and honked the horn. Shawn was up like a shot. She had been dressed and ready for a full hour. She hollered goodbye to her sleeping mom and raced out to the SUV. The two girls hugged and giggled. The ride to the lake was full of silly games, laughter, and talk.

The lake was crammed with people swimming and boats were out on the water everywhere. The public beach was covered with staked out areas where families had laid their colorful blankets and beach towels. Small children with their inflatable 'floaties' on toddled about under the scrutiny of parental supervision. Young lovers lay side-by-side on beach towels in the warm summertime sun.

Shawn and Maggie ran to a place on the beach. "Mom, Dad, this is our spot right here." Maggie and Shawn raced around leaving footprints in the sand as Maggie's parents arrived at the site. "Come on, Shawn, let's go swim."

Shawn and Maggie stripped to their swimsuits, tossing shirts and shorts, and rushed down to the edge of the water.

"Race you to the dock," Maggie said as she took off toward the floating platform.

Shawn quickly followed.

The dock was crowded with girls and boys about their age and some older. Maggie helped Shawn up onto the dock. "Told you I'd beat you."

"You cheated."

"Did not. I just started earlier." Maggie giggled.

"Hey, move over, stop hogging my space." Shawn laughed and pushed Maggie off the dock and into the water.

"I'll get you for that." Maggie sputtered as she

emerged from the lake.

Other kids they knew from school began to arrive and amidst them was Jake Michaels, a ninth grade football player. He was popular with girls and boys alike.

"Hey, Shawn," he said.

"Hi." She felt like butterflies were in her stomach.

"Are you ready for summer?"

As she turned to respond, his dark blue eyes and brown hair took her aback. For a moment, Jeremy left her mind completely. "Not really, I haven't got any plans right now, but I'm glad it's summer."

"I am, too," he said as he reached over and pushed her off the dock into the water.

She bobbed to the surface and reached up to get him to give her a hand onto the dock. "Real funny, tough boy." She jerked him into the water headfirst.

When he came up, they both laughed. He swam up to her and said, "Look over there, there's Maggie, what's she doing?"

Shawn looked and he dunked her under the water. "You dog." She sputtered as she came up for air. She surprised him and returned the dunk.

"Alright, girl, this is war." He swam over and pecked her right on her lips then swam away.

All of a sudden her world with Jeremy faded into the past. Summer had truly begun.

That evening, after a great picnic of hotdogs and chips, swimming, and playing Twister on the beach with Maggie and her family, she arrived home. She raced up the sidewalk and into the house. She stopped at the fridge, grabbed an ice-cold Coke, and then walked out onto the back porch. There, asleep, lay Blackie.

*

Blackie felt himself being lifted by his front paws. *What on earth! It's the mistress. What does she want now?*

Shawn danced a little dance with him. "Oh Blackie, It's summer, It's summer!" All Blackie got out of this conversation was…"blah, Blackie, blah, blah, blah, blah, blah, blah!" He knew though, that whatever Shawn was saying it was good because of the inflection in her voice. Also, she only danced with him on grand occasions. *Maybe I am going to get a snack, or a pat, or a toy, or a…* His doggy thoughts roamed on and on until she released him and he brought his front paws back down to the porch.

The Bassicus Angleris of East Texas
By
Vivra P. Beene

Alternating with the scenic, singing pines of East Texas are numerous equally scenic lakes. Mostly man made, but none-the-less beautiful for that, they are home to a varied selection of wild life. In summer, they are also the base for many graceful water sports.

Imagine the peaceful beauty of a sailboat scudding along, sails billowing in the gentle summer breeze, rainbow colors outlined against a cloudless azure sky.

Imagine, too, the glittering streamlined arrow of a fast moving motorboat, pulling a tanned, muscular figure on water skis, the skier executing graceful acrobatics on the surface of the water as if he were a dolphin.

These sportsmen share the waters with ducks and other waterfowl, nutrias, and of course, fish. The mention of fish brings to mind another animal that can be found in abundance on East Texas lakes. The Bassicus Angleris, commonly known as a bass angler, can be found on any lake in any season, but seems to be more prolific during the summer months. Weather does not dampen his spirits. Neither rain nor wind can daunt him. Thunder and lightning? Well, maybe.

The bass angler can be male or female. However, it is sometimes difficult to discern one from the other due to the outer covering. The difference is easier to see during the heat of the summer, when they tend to wear whatever they feel comfortable in.

For example, a prominent member of a local bass club was spotted on a lake close to Kilgore, wearing shocking-pink jogging shorts, a lime green T-shirt sporting the phrase 'Nurses do it on the floors,' bottomed off with black, leather cowboy boots. And that was a male of the species.

Transportation on the water for these creatures is as varied as their mode of dress. Dark green, flat-bottomed 'jon boats' with a low horsepower motor on the stern and little else—all the way up to eighteen-foot spear shaped speed machines with futuristic electronic gear that does all but fillet and cook the resulting catch of largemouth bass.

Their boats are slow and graceful—or swift and graceful, but is Bassicus Angleris? Picture a bass angler seated on the front decking of his boat on a swivel seat. His right foot rests on the control of an electric trolling motor that moves him along with a whisper at a mere snail's pace. He casts his line with a minimal flick of the wrist. Slowly, he reels in the line.

Graceful? Well, certainly not clumsy. Wait, he's got a bite! Standing, he jerks back to set the hook. Hitting the seat with the back of his knees, he executes an unplanned back flip, does the splits, and with action previously attributed only to contestants of Dancing with the Stars, he rights himself, still reeling in the line.

Hopefully, to make this action worthwhile, he will have at least a ten-pound bass on the end of the line. Unfortunately, he will be more likely to have hooked a long-drowned tree limb or as truly happened on one occasion, a very much live baby alligator.

Another angler, intent on 'popping' a colorful top-water lure across the surface of the lake, looked up to see he was about to collide with a menacing tree stump.

He was on the lake for fishing, not swimming, so in an effort to avoid both the stump and a swim, he put his foot over the prow of the boat to act as a buffer against the stump. Unfortunately, he overbalanced, and ended up *on* the stump, with his boat going its own merry way across the lake. He was forced to swim after all—all the way to his boat.

Bassicus Angleris is a social creature. It likes to get together with others for fishing tournaments. To study them and hear their stories, visit an East Texas lake at the end of one of these tournaments. You will hear how "I lost a big 'un, got a hundred pound test line and that sucker broke it—snapped it like it was nuthin'," and the response, "Ha, I was working hard reeling in a hawg, looked up and by gorey, that lunker had pulled me an' the boat all the way back to the boat dock!"

If you're lucky, you'll be invited to a fish fry, where you might have the honor of sampling a succulent fillet from the tournament's winning 'big bass.' A satisfying end to a captivating study of just one of the many creatures at home on the lakes of East Texas.

Autumn

The Cabin
By
Evelyn M. Byrne

Jack McKenzie needed this vacation and he loved this time of the year in the mountains. The season when the leaves transformed into their bouquet of colors and you could feel the crisp chill of winter begin to permeate the air.

He had been working non-stop for the last three years building JMJ Investigations & Security with his two partners. It had finally paid off. They were now in such high demand that they had two other private investigators working for them, and double the rest of their staff. Having everything running smoothly, he and his partners decided to each take two weeks off. Mark took his time off last month, and Joe was scheduled next month, but starting today, Jack was off to the wilderness with his tent and backpack where there were no phones, faxes, or computers for two glorious weeks.

It didn't take long for Jack to get into a routine of hiking, fishing, and just plain relaxing. He felt the stress of the last three years melt away with each passing day.

Lost in his thoughts, he stepped into a clearing, stopped dead, and stared. *What the hell? That wasn't here before*. With his background, he would never have missed seeing the fancy cabin smack-dab in the middle of the forest. *I've been traipsing through these woods for the last week and a half. I know I came this way at least once or twice. Besides, who would want a cabin in the middle of nowhere?*

The cabin looked as if it had popped out of one of

those log cabin magazines. Floor-to-ceiling glass covered the entire front of the massive two-story cabin. Its walk-around porch had a swing and some rocking chairs, plus plants everywhere.

How did they get the equipment and materials in here to even build it? I don't remember seeing a single road within a good ten miles. By helicopter? Otherwise, they would have to hike in and out every time they needed anything.

Jack walked around the building, figuring there had to be some kind of road leading in that he hadn't noticed. After circling the cabin twice, he concluded nothing but dense forest surrounded it. *There's no place to land a chopper either.* A shiver ran up his spine. *This is too damn weird.* He marched up the steps and knocked on the door. He waited a minute then made another circuit around the house, but saw no sign of anyone.

A whip-poor-will's call reminded him of the late hour. *Damn. I'll come back early tomorrow and find the owner.* He looked over his shoulder one last time, clicked on his flashlight, and headed into the darkening forest.

*

Just after sunup, Jack finished breakfast and set out through the forest. He arrived at the spot where he'd seen the cabin, only to find the clearing empty. Spinning in a circle, he scanned the clearing. *This is impossible—I know I didn't mix up the trails.* He scouted every trail he could find through the remainder of the day looking for the cabin, to no avail.

At twilight, he headed back to his campsite and passed through the clearing once again. As he stepped out of the forest, the hair on the back of his neck stood on end. There stood the magnificent cabin in all its splendor. Jack rubbed his eyes. *I know this is the same place I came to this morning. How is this possible?*

He trucked around the cabin once more looking for someone, anyone, but had no luck. Jack ran his hands through his hair. *What the hell?* With darkness closing in around him, he thought it best to head back to his campsite. He pulled a knife from his pocket and marked the trees at the edge of the clearing. Tomorrow he'd be certain.

*

Jack climbed from his tent the next morning and stretched as he inhaled deeply. *Man, the air always smells so fresh and clean after a good rain.* The ground remained wet from the overnight shower, which meant the path would probably be muddy, causing him to delay heading out for the day until just past ten. He dodged most of the puddles, yet his jeans soon got damp and muddy. Arriving at the clearing, he found it empty once again.

"No effin way!"

He checked for the notched trees at the edge of the path, rubbing them with a finger to convince himself they were there. They were. This was real. With his pounding heart and sweaty palms, he turned and practically flew back to his campsite, slipping and sliding the whole way.

Once there, he bolted into the tent and took slow deep breaths to settle his nerves.

"Get a grip Jack"

When his breathing slowed, he took out a pad of paper to make some notes, hand poised over the paper as he gathered his thoughts.

"Okay, I know I went down that trail at least four times." He scrubbed a hand through his hair. "Now, the night before last... Hmmm, was that the first time I went through in the dark? Yeah. Most nights I was already back here. Shit! This is impossible. I have to be dreaming." He threw his notepad across the tent.

For the next few minutes, he sat still, letting the sounds of the forest calm him. *Feel better now Jack?* Then leaned over and picked up his notepad. *Let's start again.*

"There was no cabin when I went there yesterday morning, but it was there again last night." The more he tried to figure it out, the more confused he got. "Damn, if I tell anyone, especially my partners, about this they will lock me up. For Christ's sake, I used to be a detective, and I'm now one of the top PI's in the field. I deal in facts and hard evidence. So let's go get some of that hard evidence."

Armed with his camera and his notes, Jack headed back to the clearing. Once there he took several pictures from different angles, making sure certain landmarks were in each picture. Then he settled himself against a tree at the edge of the clearing and waited. Each hour he took the same shots for comparison later.

As twilight crept in, the cabin began to materialize. He snapped pictures furiously, capturing the cabin as it solidified more and more. *Now, I have my proof. I'm not going crazy.*

Putting his camera back in his pack, he watched the cabin, undecided whether or not to go any closer.

Without warning, the front door opened, and light from inside the house bathed the clearing. Jack took a step back into the darkness. A tall blonde woman in a flowing dress stepped out onto the porch. Her beauty drew him from the shadows.

"Hi there." When she startled, he added, "Sorry, I didn't mean to frighten you."

She smiled. "No, I just didn't realize someone was here." Then she frowned. "You shouldn't be here. You must leave...now."

He felt it would be smarter not to mention he had been sitting here all day, or the fact that he had watched her house pop out of nowhere. "I happened upon your cabin the night before last, but no one was here. I'm camping about a mile away and thought I would stop by again tonight." He took another step toward the cabin. "This is an amazing home you have, have you lived here long?"

She sighed. "Far longer than I would like."

"If you don't like it here, why don't you move to

town?"

"Come, join me for a drink, and I'll explain it to you."

He climbed the steps and sat in one of the rockers. She disappeared into the house and returned shortly with a pitcher of lemonade with two glasses and some iced cookies. She sat on the rocker facing the one he chose.

"I was hiking in these woods almost fifteen years ago and came upon this cabin just as you did. An elderly woman lived here then. She told me how she'd been here for many years and how she could never leave. She said I had to leave before dawn or I would be trapped here like her until someone else took my place. And here I am."

"Have you ever tried to just walk out at night when the cabin is visible, like it is now?"

She snorted. "Yes, more than once, but I can never find a way out. Every time I've tried it's as if the trees close in to make a cage."

Jack stood. "Let's try it together and see if you can leave with me."

Her gaze darted around the area as if looking for someone. "Oh that's not possible. They will never let me leave until there is someone to replace me."

"Who are they?"

She didn't answer, only shook her head.

He extended his hand. "Look, it won't hurt to try."

She took it, and they went down the steps. They walked around the clearing trying to find one of the paths out, only it seemed as though the trees became so thick there was no path.

He stopped after making three trips around the cabin. "How is this possible? I know there is a trail here someplace, I used it not long ago."

He glanced over his shoulder. *Where the hell is my backpack? Where are the notched trees?* Again, he looked over his shoulder. A shiver ran up his spine. *I know I was sitting under a tree somewhere about there.*

She shrugged. "I told you...I can't leave until I am

replaced."

"There has to be some way for you to get out."

She shook her head. "I really don't know. The old woman warned me but I didn't listen. The minute the sun dawned, she vanished. I've been stuck in this cursed place ever since. I have read bits of her journals telling how she tried to leave but with no luck.

They walked around a few more times.

Suddenly, she jerked her hand from his, pushed him, and yelled, "Hurry! They're coming. Get into the trees. Run!"

Jack stumbled and dove for the path that materialized in front of him the moment she released his hand. He rolled behind a gigantic pine, climbed to his feet, and cautiously peered out from behind it. *It feels like something tried to stop me.*

From his position, Jack watched as three columns of light appeared around the woman. He looked down and saw his backpack lying against the tree across the path. *Crap. I need that.*

He shot across the path, landing behind the oak he had sat against most of the day. He snagged the strap of his backpack, and yanked it behind the tree.

Every hair on his body stood at attention. *I need to get out of here and I need to do it now.* Staying in the shadow of the trees, Jack moved farther away from the clearing until he could no longer see the light from the cabin. He dug his flashlight out of his pack, turned it on, and sprinted back to camp.

Once inside his tent, it took him what seemed like forever to slow his heart rate. *What the fuck is going on? Is someone playing some kind of sick joke?*

He pulled out his camera and notes. He flipped the camera on and glanced through the pictures. *Well if they are, it is a pretty elaborate scheme. It's not a hologram, because I sat on the porch.*

After examining the pictures a few more times, he put

the camera and notes away in his backpack and climbed into his sleeping bag. *This may be the biggest mystery ever, and no one is going to believe it. Hell, I wouldn't believe me if I hadn't been there.*

Continue the adventure with Jack http://goo.gl/UBtTi

Escape
By
Lynn Hobbs

Light as a feather, she took a step off the concrete walkway. Mindful of possible discovery, her eyes glanced in all directions. *Great, no one is here. I can finally do this.* Sheer excitement dared her to walk farther. Her heart raced from a sudden adrenalin rush, like she hadn't experienced for years.

Gusts of wind blew a salty sea smell into her nostrils. Gulls walked on the sand, their loud screeches increasing in volume at her approach. She treasured the moment, enjoying the breeze. It whipped her hair about with a sudden icy chill only the fall winds could bring.

Proud and still, she stood, absorbed in the bounty of rewards the Gulf Coast offered, until her senses filled. A few steps closer to the white caps of water, licking at the sand, and her desire to return to the ocean was satisfied. Seaweed littered the area—a stringy mass of goop to avoid.

She stumbled on a large, half-hidden shell that protruded from the sand, making her footing that much more precarious. A flex of muscles and generous arch of her back helped, in an attempt to loosen her old aching joints.

Voices floated down concrete stairs, leading to the beach. Startled at the intrusion of others, her body jerked. Her ears strained, her eyes opened wide, and she tried not to panic.

They're close, whoever it is. I have to hide. Can't let them find me. A quick scan across the area did offer relief.

Hmm, yes, perfect. In a hurry, she eased herself down onto the sand, behind a cluster of granite boulders. Weary, she remained silent.

*

"Jack, come on, let's wiggle our toes in the sand."

"It's cold out here," he blurted, and crossed his arms over his chest.

"Adventure calls," Sherry yelled into the wind. Undeterred, she slipped off her shoes and skipped across the water, while waves swept over her ankles.

"We didn't even bring a towel, Sherry. You'll be a muddy mess."

"I *won't* waste our solitude here." She gave a mischievous grin.

Jack grabbed her into his arms, as he spoke in a deliberate deep voice, "Frankly, Scarlett, I don't give a...hoot...about wasting this beach, *either.*"

"Oh, Rhett, that was *not* how it went in the movie," Sherry gave her best Southern accent, followed by infectious laughter. He swung her around, laughed, and looked her right in the eye.

"Alright, we can stay, but let's find someplace to sit down, out of this cold wind."

Jack whistled a merry tune while they strolled along.

"Happy?"

"Yes, my de-ah," his new Southern drawl kicked in, "I bask in the exhilarated elements of our favorite rendezvous."

Sherry threw her arms up in the air, "Enough, Mr. Twain, I can't take anymore."

"Okay," he grinned, "Remember the granite boulders the U.S. Corp of Engineers placed here along the sea wall?"

"Do I ever. The Corp of Engineers owns the sea wall and the Galveston Park Board manage it."

Arm in arm they continued, until the distance between themselves and the boulders disappeared. Jack helped her sit, first, before he sprawled out. Careful to position both their backs against the natural windbreak, each stretched their legs out on the sand. Sherry leaned her head onto his shoulder as they sat close together.

"I'm glad you insisted we make this trip, especially after the summer season is over. I treasure this privacy."

"So do I, Jack. Galveston has many fond memories for me. I used to walk across the top of the sea wall when I was younger. We camped out here a lot, in those days."

"Your childhood and mine are different as night and day. I think because I grew up in the north, with all the ice and snow, I can't get enough of this coast." He took a deep breath and glanced upward. Sea gulls flew in with their piercing calls, landed for a brief moment, only to fly further inland. Another flock of shorebirds, the smaller sandpipers, scattered about the edge of the water on tiny legs.

Sherry sat upright. "I've always loved being born and raised in Houston with Galveston nearby. As a child, I'd play games with my cousins on this beach. Wow, those days were full of excited activities and laughter and noise." She paused, "Mom had sixteen brothers and sisters and everyone was married and had kids. At least, four or five of the families would spend the weekend here, during good weather. We'd sing together around a huge bonfire at night, while the men cooked on their portable grills. Later, I was amazed when my uncles wore hip-waders and would simply walk out into the ocean, stand still and fish."

"I think it's against the law to have bonfires or camp out here, now," Jack replied.

"It is, and I noticed the signs warning not to fish off the jetties, or even stand on them."

"What's the jetties?"

"See that row of boulders coming out from the shore and going straight out to sea for nearly a mile? That is just one of the jetties, and we used to climb all over them. It was not so perilous, if you watched the tide. When the tide is in, waves splash water across the top of the rocks and the green algae that grows there become slimy and wet. No one can move, without sliding, which could prove fatal. Tides out, the wind dries the algae, and you can walk to the end of the jetties. The top surface is jagged and rough, though, you have to be careful where you step," Sherry recalled, "but the fishing and the view are so worth it."

"I can see why they put warning signs up."

"My Dad used to bring fresh oysters, still in their shells, home from Galveston. He would have a huge, croaker sack full and shuck them in our garage. I was about eight years old when he taught me how to eat them raw. The first one he handed me, I swallowed, and it came back up, completely whole. He laughed and said I had to chew it up. Later, we'd dip them in a horseradish concoction to enjoy raw with crackers, and Mom refused to join us. Now, I wouldn't dare eat oysters unless they are fried. Yum, such a treat! Yes, this place brings back a lot of good memories," she gushed.

From the other side of the boulders, a low moan clearly sounded, as a majestic cold, wind thrust down upon the beach.

Sherry refrained her reminiscing and froze. "Did you hear something?"

"No, only the wind."

"It was not *the wind*."

"Okay, *Miss Imagination*. It was a shipwrecked *sailor in distress*, hanging onto a plank, eighty feet out at sea, and *shouting* for help."

She frowned and turned to squarely face Jack, balled up her fist, and promptly hit him on his arm.

"Babe, I couldn't resist." He grabbed and kissed her, before she realized what he was going to do.

Tide began rolling in, and a massive gust of wind, covered them from head to toe, with a mist of salty seawater.

"Yuck," Sherry sputtered, as she stood up, and

attempted to wipe her face.

Jack raised his lanky self up and grinned at Sherry. He lightly caressed her cheek with his hand, "My, can you ever *talk*, girl." He smoothed the windblown hair back from her face, and held her in his arms.

Disturbed by hearing a long groan, Sherry eased away. *I know what I heard, but I'm not about to tell him.* "And can you ever *whistle*. What was that tune a while ago?" Sherry stood aloof.

"Two bottles of beer on the wall, two bottles of beer, take one away…"

Sherry interrupted, "I've heard of it. We did something else where I grew up, the name song."

"What in the world are you talking about? What is the *name* song?"

"Use my name, Sherry. It would go like this; Sherry, Sherry, boe berry, boe nana, fana, fo ferry—Sherry!"

"Man, what a song." Jack sighed, and looked away.

"Listen to this, we'll sing it with your name," Sherry rattled on.

"No, I don't want to hear it."

"Oh, Jack. It would be fun to sing with you, come on."

He kicked sand into the air with his shoe, and danced his fingers across her arm. Raising his eyebrows in expectation, he lightly kissed her on her forehead. "We are all alone," he mumbled into her ear.

"Stop it, Jack, big difference between animal instinct and real love. Someday I'll be married and it *will* be special."

Jack cocked his head to the side and spoke slow, "You are *not* loose with your affections, like other girls I have dated."

Her response was halted by another moan. "I hear it again. Jack, something is on the other side of the boulders."

"Well, come on, let's check it out."

Sherry beat him around to the other side. "Oh," she gasped, as a head rose up, and gave her a pleading look. "Oh, Jack," Sherry whimpered, and a bark could be heard along the beach.

"What?" he said from behind her.

"Jack, it's a cocker spaniel, with auburn hair, and…no collar." She gingerly picked up the dog and wrapped her arms around it.

He took the dog from her and circled his other arm around Sherry's waist. Distant sounds of wind chimes jingled in the breeze, and beckoned them up to the souvenir shops, nearby.

"If we hurry, we can make the ferry to Port Bolivar." He smiled at Sherry and tightened his grip on the dog as it wagged its tail.

Sweet Cherie Pie
By
Judith Victoria Douglas

After my record thirty-third blind date calamity, I embedded my so-called lucky charm into a wad of my nephew's Silly Putty and gave it my best Texas quarterback toss…out into the Hudson.

No more lucky charm, and no more blind dates. I'll have to replace Andy's Silly Putty on my next visit to Roanoke. He could fill the new one with spaghetti, too, if he wants.

The faint aroma from my doggy bag reminded me of the long evening's misfortune. I retrieved it from the bench to shuffle toward home, feeling mighty low.

It has to be me. She was lovely, but too practiced —a polished New York professional.

Cold shivers ran up my back, shaking my shoulders. I wasn't sure if it was an early autumn chill, or my mood. It generated a myriad of thoughts.

I guess I'll never blend in, even with these Armani suits. I'll start wearing my western-cut suits again. Without an employer to tell me how to dress, I could do that.

I kicked an imaginary rock with my tasseled Gucci loafer. My situation fell heavy as an old cloak over my shoulders.

Ah, get real, Joe, you chump. She brushed you off because the big cutbacks locked you out of the financial district. Gawd, she probably makes more than I ever did. Wonder if she saw me *as the gold-digger? Katy's not going to like my report on her "best choice" for me.*

At least the chef accepted my compliments. Nice touch, the free dessert. Guess I'll have hers for breakfast. Did I look desperate, taking the leftovers? I can't believe she paid the bill. How low can a guy get?

I sighed deeply as I reached the corner before hailing a cab.

It'll be the subway soon.

Just the thought made me claustrophobic. I stopped the cabbie before he put his foot to the pedal, handing him a couple of bucks. I had to walk—get lost in the night's crowds. The noise and bright lights were good. It kept me from thinking too much.

*

A week later, after two curt interviews and nowhere else to go, I got a call from my best friend and old teammate, Jake. I hoped he didn't have another prospect for me, unless it was job related. Before he could get into it, I spoke.

"You chose better than I did, Holtster. Being a doctor with lots of opportunities is better than being a financial whiz kid with no place to go."

"Feeling sorry for yourself? Don't worry so much, Magnetti. You can always stay with us 'til you get on your feet, but I think I've got just the cure."

"This one's *the one*, bro. Take it from your doctor friend, the guy who knows you best."

Gotta be better than my sister, Katy's, picks. My thought only allowed a moment for that disgruntled exasperation that comes from friends trying too hard to fix your life.

"Okay," I mumbled, "here we go again."

I hesitated, slapping my forehead. My hand slowly rolled down over my face as I listened. He gave his best sales pitch ever. I finally gave in.

"Yeah, all right, okay, but only because she's from Texas. And this is the last time. What is it with you married folks, anyway? Just because I didn't have an old girlfriend to transplant to the big city like you did doesn't mean I want one now. Hell, I'm jobless. The next time someone calls to arrange a blind date, or if this one's as bad as the others, he'll be put at the top of my Hit List."

"Just make it apple pie this time, goofus. That's my *favorite*."

"I don't know. Those juicy red globs looked pretty funny dripping down all over your face the last time."

"That was to celebrate, a long time ago. And I still hate cherry pie, thanks to you. It's only okay because we're still friends."

"Yeah…best ever…for life, buddy. Just remember that when you have my pie all over your face again."

*

This time, I went as the down-home boy. Western-cut suit with boots, Texas college, Texas football, love pickup trucks, horses, and Waylon. Still miss my old dog. When she entered the room, I almost whooped like an old rodeo clown.

She was a real Texas beauty. No big city polish, just warmth and flavor like biscuits and gravy or…hot cherry pie.

Dinner was a typical New York steak, as close to home as I could get. She was Texas friendly, trying something more New Yorkish, as she put it. I made a few suggestions of my own favorites.

The conversation was all about the big state we both called home. She had some good stories to tell of recent events I'd missed. It made me homesick, but it was the first time I'd laughed on a New York date. She smiled big at my response, and I melted.

Cherie. Sweet Cherie pie.

I felt like the luckiest Joe on the planet, and it didn't matter what state I was in. She liked me, and I liked her. We seemed two peas from the same patch.

We did it again, many times…the dinners, but also great walks in Central Park for long chats, eventually holding hands. The quiet moments were nice, too, comfortable and cozy, like thick socks on a winter's cold floor.

We visited several museums, attended a play with a couple of my friends, a concert courtesy of my elderly neighbor, got guest invitations for a movie premier from an old colleague, saw all the national monuments and landmarks, then went crazy shopping like tourists. It was fun, even the deli lunches, hot dog stands, and feeding the pigeons.

We watched *Good Morning, America* on my small hand-held set sitting on a bench across the street below their big window. I brought my dad's binoculars so she could see up close.

She talked openly with strangers in the crowd. Some finally warmed to her, but she made the cutest face when they didn't. One older lady shared her hot cocoa after borrowing the binoculars, and we all laughed about our little early morning adventure.

My girl had the most beautiful, heart-warming laugh.

I'd never truly seen this amazing city before. It opened my eyes to see it through hers. No wonder I felt I'd never fit in. I would always be a tourist here.

Then she had to go back home…to Austin…my alma mater town. There were some exciting exchanges about familiar locations, past experiences, and areas we each liked. It was all so good until she revealed her real purpose for her visit. I should have known. Everything was too perfect. She confessed during our last, most intimate moments.

She was on sabbatical, that was true, but it was for recovery from a long, hard bout of chemo. She assured me the cancer was gone, but there were no guarantees. She said she'd had a grand time; it wouldn't have been the same without me and made me promise to keep in touch.

My heart sank.

I promised myself I wouldn't let her go, even as I

watched the plane disappear, but I was in that hard place nobody likes to be. The rock in my stomach didn't help. It'd been the best weeks of my life. I didn't want it to end.

*

Days of sitting in darkness followed, listening to Waylon's saddest refrains.

I started pacing the apartment I was about to lose, unsure if I could be so bold. I couldn't let it end, but my jobless status put indecision where gusto wanted to reign.

No one knows what tomorrow will bring, I kept telling myself. We're not born with a guarantee stamped on our bottoms, and things *can* change for the better. I had to believe that, or I couldn't go through with it.

Jerking up the phone in desperation, I called in a promise made years ago.

Then I called her. We talked a long time.

*

Later, with my package next to me on the seat, I called Jake from the cab on my way to his uptown apartment.

"I have something to ask of you, bro," I said soft and slow so he'd know I was serious.

"I wondered how things were going. It's been over a month."

I heard the concern in his voice.

"I think I need a new lucky charm."

"Did you lose that old football charm you stole from your sister's bracelet?" He sounded puzzled.

"Something like that. I was thinking maybe this time something measured in—carats."

"You got a job!" He was elated.

"Sure did," I said without fully explaining. After a pause I added, "And I've got pie."

The Cheer of Autumn
by
Jeannie Faulkner Barber

"Some people swore the house was haunted." I recalled Mother's **words when my** sister and I would beg her to tell us how she talked Daddy into buying it anyway.

I sat in the porch swing of my old home place and watched the autumn leaves appear to leap from their branches. They twisted and twirled in little pirouettes like tiny ballerinas before tiptoeing to the ground. The multihued pageantry of amber, jade, and maroon always fascinated us as little girls. Daddy's raked up piles were perfect for practicing our tumbling acts.

The day dawned beautiful and bright, like my sister, Kerry. Only weeks after her death, how could I smile, function, even exist? I shut my eyes and wrapped my fingers around the hot cup of cocoa. Tears streamed down and landed on my sweater like tiny footprints. The oncologist's horrendous words roared again, his prediction correct. *Cancer—now it's my turn to deal with the beast.* My stomach rumbled like the snarl of a mother dog and I fought back the nausea.

"Aunt Kim, are you alright?"

Absorbed in sorrow, I hadn't heard my eight-year-old niece approach. I quickly wiped away the tears, yet sure my red, Rudolf nose remained. "I'm fine, Maggie. What do you have, sweetheart?"

She offered out a cardboard box. "It's yours. Read the name."

"I see, but there's no return address. Who's it from?"

"My mama."

Trembling, I swallowed hard and took off the lid. "Maggie, this is…"

"It's your pom-pom, Aunt Kim."

"How? I mean, I thought I lost it the night we won State ten years ago."

The wrinkled strips of silver and blue tinsel sparkled like the wink from an old friend. I touched a strand of paper. It resembled my hair after a home permanent—a bad one.

Maggie sat down beside me and giggled. "You left it."

I loved her contagious, sweet laughter, but when it became uncontrollable, I started to worry. *Was this an innocent, juvenile attempt to grieve her mother's death?*

As though she read my thoughts, the laughter stopped. Arms crossed, a serious expression colored her face. "Mama got mad at you for the kiss you stole from Logan Reeves, the quarterback."

"What? Logan kissed me; I did not kiss him. Besides, Kerry never liked jocks. She wouldn't care if…"

"Let me finish, Aunt Kim." *Now I felt like the child.*

"Mama said she found it between the bleachers after everyone left to go to the victory bonfire. She wanted to burn it, but loved you too much. So, she hid it in her hope chest. Last year, after we found out about her cancer, she swore me to secrecy and told me the whole story. We laughed and cried then she made me promise to give it to you after, well, you know."

"Oh sweetheart, I'm sorry you've carried this burden around so long." I fought back the tears once more.

"Don't be sad, Aunt Kim. Mama said we should celebrate her life, relive all the funny, secret, and unforgettable memories you shared as twins." A small hand patted my knee. "Can we go in make me a cup of cocoa, too? It's chilly out here."

I harvested new strength from Maggie, and as we walked into the house, the precious pom-pom cradled in my arms, I whispered under my breath, "Rah, rah, Kerry."

'Tis the Season

Seasons of Life

Yellow Bus
By
Gay Ingram

Yellow bus lumbers down my country road
slows and pauses at my drive
the driver cranes his neck
looking for slow-footed passengers
then picks up speed and drives on by

I see as if yesterday
my tow-headed youngster dashing for his ride
knapsack a-flying with each leap
eager to venture into life
beyond our little world

now somewhere across town
he sits, morning paper set aside
his own toddler dandled on his knee
past and future come together
as he watches a yellow school bus lumber by

Twirl Mom's Revenge
by
Kimberli O'Brien

Crash!

All Vera could think about as she floored the accelerator was how her baby had been wronged. This was *her* daughter's moment to shine, *her* daughter's time in the spotlight. It's what they'd been working so hard for since Patricia was seven years old. Now, that dreadful Mary Lou Watson and her mother Gladys had stolen the dream right out from under their feet. In Vera's humble opinion, Gladys should have been wearing a scarlet letter to show the world just how much of a good, Christian woman she absolutely was *not*.

Patricia Young was born March 8, 1950. She was nicknamed Patty by her doting father when she was just a baby. She started twirling at age seven. Her mother knew immediately that Patty had a God-given talent. She encouraged her to practice hard and strive to be the best she could be. At age nine, she twirled at her fourth grade talent show. Patty fell in love with the spotlight. From then on, if there was a festival, talent show, or any kind of public event needing entertainment, you could bet that Patricia Young would be there with her batons.

At age ten, Patty went to her first football game. At the half-time ceremonies, she sat, eyes glued on the field, watching the band and twirlers. "Mother, what's the difference between the twirlers and the one in the very front all by herself?"

"Well," Vera said, "they are all twirlers, but the girl in the front is the drum major. She leads the whole band."

"Wow. That's what I'm going to be one day."

Vera hugged her daughter and relished this moment as Patty sat there in a small high school football stadium, building dreams she would strive the rest of her adolescent years to attain.

*

February of her sophomore year, Patty was in the cafeteria when she noticed a new girl at the end of the line. She was very beautiful, with her red hair fixed in a stylish flip and wearing a department store dress. Patty went to her and introduced herself. "Hi, I'm Patty. You must be new here."

Looking Patty up and down, she said, "I'm Mary Lou. Is that dress *homemade*?"

Patty wasn't sure whether this girl was being mean or just curious, so she gave her the benefit of the doubt. "Actually, I did make it myself."

"Well, I wouldn't be caught dead in something that wasn't from Sears." Mary Lou turned her back on Patty.

Poor Patty was crushed and tears started falling, though she willed them not to. She was in a daze the rest of the day.

When she got home from school, Vera could tell something was wrong. "What's wrong, Patty?"

Patty just shook her head.

"Patricia, you tell me what happened at school right now. Your eyes are all puffy and red so don't tell me there is nothing wrong. I love you and I can tell when you're upset."

"Okay, Mother, but it's no big deal. There's a new girl at school named Mary Lou, and she made fun of my dress is all. I'm okay."

Vera sighed. "Darling, you are beautiful and talented. To hell with whatever anyone else thinks, especially someone who doesn't even know you."

Patty gasped. Her mother had never used that kind of language before. She was smiling on the inside just knowing her mother loved her so much to get that worked

129

up over something she was almost over anyway.

In late spring of junior year, twirler tryouts were held just as they were every spring.

"Are you *really* going to wear that?"

Patty jumped up. She had been so engrossed in mentally going through her routine she didn't hear Mary Lou slip in.

This time, Patty stood up for herself, "As a matter of fact I am. And yes, I did make this. I'm also proud of the sequins and fringe I added all by myself. That's not an easy task, but you wouldn't know since you obviously have everything handed to you on a silver platter." It felt great to finally tell Mary Lou exactly what she thought.

"My mother bought my costume from Macy's in New York." Mary Lou tossed her baton in the air and missed when she went to catch it.

"Well, I hope she bought you some talent to go with it," Patty said and stormed out of the room feeling stronger and more self-confident than ever.

When the list of twirlers who made the line was posted, *Patricia Young* was on it. Down at the bottom was Mary Lou Watson—*Alternate*.

Patty hugged her mother and said, "Next year I'll be leading the band."

"You sure will, sweetheart."

Patty knew she would only have to put up with Mary Lou if another one of the twirlers got injured or sick. She said a silent prayer for the other girls to stay healthy all year.

Junior year passed with Patty trying to steer clear of Mary Lou, and Mary Lou doing everything she could to hurt Patty. Patty prayed for strength to deal with the girl's aggression. Most of the time, Patty could just ignore the comments, but every once in a while she would snap back at Mary Lou.

"You just think you're so great because you made twirler, and I'm stuck being an alternate, don't you? Well,

I'm going to be the drum major next year. You better get used to looking at my behind because that's all you'll be seeing while I'm leading the band," Mary Lou scoffed.

"There is no way *you* will be drum major! You weren't even good enough to twirl this year. What makes you think you're qualified to lead the entire band?"

"My mother hired a private teacher for me, and I've been practicing. Plus, Mother promised me she would do whatever it takes." She stalked off leaving Patty to wonder what in the world *that* meant.

*

A couple of weeks before tryouts, Vera had some Band Booster donation money she'd collected and needed to drop off with the band director's wife. She drove over to their house and saw a shiny, blue Corvette parked out by the curb. Vera knocked on the door and saw the curtains move, but no one answered. She thought that was odd since it appeared the Johnsons had company. Since she needed to go by the grocery store, she decided to swing back by afterwards.

Inside the local market, Vera noticed Alice. "Hey, Alice. I just stopped by your house to drop off the donation money, but no one answered the door."

"Oh, Paul is sick in bed right now. He wanted some undisturbed rest for a while and asked if I would take little Jessie here and leave for a bit. Jessie's colic has been acting up lately so we are headed to my mother's for the day."

"Aww, your poor little baby. Well, I hope Jessie and Paul get to feeling better soon. Here's that money. Have a good day." Vera turned to leave.

"You, too, and tell Patty I said good luck at tryouts," Alice said with a smile.

"I'll tell her. Thank you."

On tryout day, Vera pulled her Buick up to the high school. She noticed that same blue Corvette she'd seen at the Johnson's house now parked at the school. "That's weird," she said aloud. "The Johnsons don't have that kind of money."

Then she turned her thoughts to Patty. It was the day she'd dreamed of since that night she'd watched the band and vowed she would be drum major.

After Patty's turn was over, she rushed into her mother's arms. "I did the best I've ever done. I got it. I know I got it."

"I'm sure you did, darling. You've worked so hard for this."

Mr. Johnson tacked the list up and the girls rushed to scan it for their names. There was a scream.

"What? No!" It was Patty's voice.

Another high-pitched voice was heard, "I got it, Mother. Thank you, thank you. I'm drum major!"

Vera steered Patty away from the crowd and tried to calm her down. "It's going to be okay, Patty. Your future is full of…"

Patty quickly cut her off. "She told me this would happen. That's why she was thanking her mother."

"What?" Vera didn't understand what her daughter was saying.

"Mary Lou told me her mother promised she would be drum major. She said she would do whatever she had to do to make it happen."

Then something clicked. The car. The band director. Vera went to one of her friends and asked, "Do you know whose Corvette that is outside?"

"Oh yes, that's Gladys Watson's car. Isn't it beautiful? I heard her husband gave it to her about a month ago before leaving on his business trip," came the reply.

Curious, Vera pressed her, "Business trip? What kind of business is he in?"

"I heard he's a banker and travels a lot overseas. That's where he is now. Paris, I believe. He's been there for a whole month."

That's all Vera needed to hear. She knew exactly how

Gladys had made good on her promise to Mary Lou.

She was irate to say the least. Vera marched straight to her car, got in, and hit the gas pedal with a lead foot.

Crash!

Little blue pieces of fiberglass went flying. Vera put the car in reverse, backed up, and slammed into the car again. She decided that wasn't quite good enough and did it one more time.

"What are you doing? Are you crazy? What have you done to my new car?"

Vera was in the insanity zone. It took her a minute to realize there was yelling coming from somewhere.

She jumped out and got in Gladys' face.

"Your daughter has no right to be drum major, and you know it. She didn't earn it. Your mattress skills did."

There was a loud, collective gasp from the crowd gathered to watch the small town cat fight.

Gladys said, "I have no idea what you're talking about."

"I saw you at Paul Johnson's house when he was supposedly sick in bed. And don't you tell me you were bringing him chicken soup."

The crowd gasped again. Alice Johnson looked at Paul and said, "Is it true?"

He broke out into a sweat and started to stammer, "Alice...I..."

Alice slapped him across the face and stomped off, baby Jessie on her hip.

Gladys folded her arms across her chest. "Well, it doesn't make any difference what I may or may not have been doing at the Johnson's house. Your daughter, in her hand sewn rags, isn't good enough to shine my daughter's shoes, much less lead the band."

Vera instinctively clenched her fists and gritted her teeth. "You can insult me all you want, but don't you dare insult my little girl that way!" Vera's fist collided with Gladys' face.

Caught off guard, Gladys stumbled over a bench and fell to her knees.

Bringing her hand to her face she said, "You broke my nose. You, you witch!" She got up and charged at Vera, grabbed her hair, and pulled out a big chunk.

Vera fought back, clawing at Gladys' face and kicking her. They fell to the ground in a blur of flying hair, scratching, and rolling around, with bursts of swearing mingled in.

The police arrived and pulled them apart.

As they were being led to separate police cars, Vera yelled, "I'm going to the School Board and demand another tryout where the band director is not a judge!"

Gladys said, "Oh yeah? Well, this had nothing to do with the band director. It's your daughter's lack of talent!"

Vera broke free of the policeman who was holding her and ran to give Gladys one final piece of her mind, actually, one final punch in the face, which knocked out two of her teeth.

"That's what you get when you disrespect a twirl mom's daughter," Vera said.

A Princess in Her Own Right
by
Kimmie Easley

Once upon a time, there was a young girl born into a humble but loving family. Her mother often called her beautiful. The day she was born her father dubbed her Princess. There had never been, and would never be, a shade of blue to compare to her sparkling, round eyes.

Princess's skin was soft and her cheeks stayed a subtle pink. Mother rocked Princess back and forth as she listened to the birds share their appreciation for the warm spring day. Father sat close by stroking Princess's soft, golden locks, mesmerized by the sun that came in through the window and bounced off of her fair head.

Princess went on to become a bubbly toddler. She loved frilly dresses, shoes with a heel, and polka-dotted bows in her hair. Princess pushed her favorite baby doll around in a stroller by day, and brushed her long, flowing hair by night. She loved her baby and would spend hours making ponytails and braids in her dolly's hair. When Mother would do Princess's hair, she made sure her baby doll matched so they could be twins.

The years would pass and Princess began to come into her own. The dresses were passed over for jeans and t-shirts. The heels were tossed aside for flip-flops and sneakers. Baby dolls were put on shelves and replaced with sports equipment and skateboards. Her hair was still long and soft, but now a shade or two darker. Mother protected her with a fierce intensity, and Father treasured her every moment.

Princess grew to be a very sensitive little girl with her

heart her strongest asset, always putting the needs of others before her own. Many called her beautiful. Her eyes danced as her rosy cheeks swelled when she smiled. Princess' hair was stunning and drew attention everywhere she went. But one day her entire world would change.

After her morning shower, she called for Mother. Mother rushed through the bathroom door to find her daughter holding out two fistfuls of hair. Princess sat and cried as Mother held her close and whispered a promise only a mother could keep. "We'll come out stronger on the other side, my beautiful Princess."

Next would come countless doctor visits, specialist appointments, labs, and tests involving scary machines. Mother and Father were in awe at the strength Princess displayed as she lost the majority of her once unparalleled tresses. She never shed a tear as she was given a diagnosis of *Alopecia Areata*. The doctor explained this would be a lifelong disease, and there was no guarantee she would ever again have a full head of hair.

Mother tried to read her daughter's face for a hint of emotion, expecting to see pain or anger. Instead, she saw Princess's wheels begin to turn. Mother knew that look all too well, and her heart began to stir.

Later that night, Princess asked to speak to Mother and Father before snuggling into her bed. Her smile was huge, as the cheeks confirmed, and the oceans of blue danced in her eyes as she enlightened them on how she wanted to raise money for children with alopecia. She couldn't hide her enthusiasm as she explained how she wanted to help educate others on what it meant to have the illness, and she needed to show people that hair did not equal beauty.

Mother and Father smiled through the tears as they looked at Princess. She no longer wanted to cover her bare patchy head. She didn't look exactly like the other children in the neighborhood, and there was no doubt society would continue to smirk and stare.

Mother and Father knew none of that mattered any longer because there she stood in all her glory, a Princess in her own right.

The Woman in the Wall Paper
By
Simon Lang

When I was in high school, I remember getting a delicious shudder of horror reading about the notorious noblemen who used to shut up their wives (sweethearts, mistresses, mothers-in-law, secretaries, Avon ladies, scrubwomen, whatever) in some little alcove of the castle and then, while singing insanely, wall them in brick by brick until they were completely enclosed. Their skeletons were found decades, sometimes centuries, later. Thank goodness, I used to say to myself, turning the page, we don't have *that* sort of thing going on any more.

Until some genius thought up do-it-yourself wallpaper.

Now, I certainly don't think of myself as another Martha Stewart, or Mrs. Clean, or anything like that. I'm reasonable. I figure I'll never make the cover of *Good Housekeeping*, but then I won't sink to the level of *Zookeeper International*, either, so I'm okay with that. But I do have this propensity for trying to make things look good, better, and better'n'at, so I decided to wallpaper my dining room.

When I undertook this insane scheme, we lived in a lovely home in a picture-book village in Connecticut, right on the Shoreline. All the houses looked like magazine ads (except ours), and I thought wallpapering our dining room was a positive step toward 'fitting in.'

Looking back, I am reminded of the line from the film, "My Cousin Vinny," when Marisa Tomei, playing his lady friend, sarcastically tells the outrageously-garbed New Jersey lawyer Vinny, just prior to his appearance in an Old South court of Law, "Yeah, babe, *you blend.*"

He didn't.

We didn't blend, either. Maybe it was our twenty kids of various colors and handicaps, maybe it was our two friendly mutts. Maybe it was me. Who knows?

I was hoping wallpaper would help.

Because the dining room had an elegant off-white wainscoting, I bought several rolls of delicately-embossed French wallpaper, in a pattern of 'faded' peach-and-sand stripes and pale pink roses with shadowy-green leaves. It was perfect! And because I had done a good job wallpapering several rooms in each of the many homes we had owned, I felt like a pro.

That was my First Mistake.

My Second mistake was trying to do it with only one helper, my darling daughter, Gret. The family still living at home had mysteriously disappeared, so we decided to do it ourselves. I quickly found out that it is possible for a person to put up French wallpaper with one helper, only if that helper is a professional paperhanger and/or a really talented octopus.

I also discovered that French wallpaper tends to roll back up, at the same time tearing itself into neat little strips the exact width of the embossed stripes. Some of them rolled up nice and tight, some were lazier, others were having none of it, and pretended to have fainted; so they all hung at different eye levels.

My wall looked like a really bad home perm, two hours before the Homecoming Dance.

As for me, I felt like the grave robber who had broken the seals on all the Qumran Scrolls at the same time, and watched them spring open and roll themselves up at will. The only difference was, those scrolls didn't have lots of nice, gooey wallpaper paste all over one whole side of them. For the first time in my life, I began to feel a deep compassion for Indiana Jones and his ilk.

Being brave and foolhardy (accent on the word 'fool'), I leapt into the fray and began trying to attach the pretty little rolls to the wall by main force and motherly speed, slapping here, smoothing there, leveling another place. Somehow, something went awfully wrong.

What I didn't know was that the charming French wallpaper, with exquisite Gallic irony, had been patiently waiting for me to come close enough. Before you could say, "For the love of God, Montresor!" it reached out and grabbed me, and I found myself glued to most of the paper scrolls, the wainscoting, the hardwood floor, and the wall—all at the same time.

However, having come this far, I was not about to give up. While Gret kept valiantly peeling me off the wall, I kept slapping up scrolls with my free hand at a rate alarming even to me.

Right about the middle of it all, my phone rang and someone tried to sell me something—I don't remember exactly what it was—but I do recall how scared she sounded when I grabbed the phone with a gluey hand, laughing maniacally and shouted, "Woman in the wall! Woman in the wall!" (Try it sometime; it really scares the bejeebers out of telemarketers.) The phone didn't ring again for the rest of the day.

It didn't dare.

It came as something of a shock, a few hours later, to find the dining room actually papered in nice, even stripes, and that wallpaper paste truly *does* come off the floor (wainscoting, skin, clothing, floor, chandelier.)

The whole family, including my Beloved, magically reappeared as soon as we cleaned up the mess, ourselves, and the tools. They admired the job we had done, and talked about how beautiful it looked, and how clever we were, and all that Good-Guy-Talk that people give you, who didn't hang around to help. I wanted to shout, "Yeah, let's see how you like it, when *you're* being wallpapered to death!" But I didn't; I kept my own counsel and said only, "Thank you," and "Eat your dinners before they get cold." And I smiled a lot.

But I found myself wondering, every now and again, just how many rolls of French wallpaper it would take to slap 'em *all*—including our 'exclusive neighbors'—up against the wall, just for a couple of days, while Gret and I sat in the charming French dining room smiling at each other, enjoying the peace and quiet, and sharing a nice cool bottle of Amontillado.

Mother Remembers
By
Kimmie Easley

Mother leaned in for a quick kiss on the Princess's cheek as she made her nightly rounds long after the family had gone to bed. Princess was snuggled with her best friend, Blueberry Bear. Mother remembered the day Princess received the old tattered bear from the hospital staff. She was so thin and tiny, curled up in the bed on wheels. The bear brought a smile to her pale face. That was six years ago. Although Princess displayed strength Mother was sure she would not possess herself, Blueberry was never far out of arm's reach.

Mother stood watching Princess sleep, snuggling the old bear. The sight made her think about how not long ago, she would stroke Princess's hair as part of their bedtime routine. Mother would move the strands of soft honey colored hair from her face.

Mother felt weak remembering the earlier years. Kneeling on the floor, looking at Princess, she thought about the day her precious daughter was born. Father was so excited when he saw the head full of hair on his beautiful gift from God. He placed Princess in Mother's arms, swaddled in a blanket with a pink and blue striped newborn cap. Mother touched the soft curls peeking out from the hem.

The little things turned into treasures, buried deep within Mother's soul, not knowing how she would come to rely on them in years to come. Mother held Princess and wet her hair with a damp washcloth. She gently lathered in the *Johnson & Johnson's* chamomile and lavender shampoo, inhaling the captivating scent. Mother knew this is what heaven must be like.

Mother collected large, beautiful bows adorned with feathers, beads and gems. Princess would wear the bows with her most adorable outfits. Her hair curled at the ends, and her bangs rested perfectly at her brow. Princess would spend her summers playing in the grass, letting her hair bounce in a way Mother can still see when she closes her eyes. Tears well as Mother remembers Princess running with open arms hair bobbing up and down and her blue eyes radiating brighter than the summer sun.

"Mother?" Princess asked, bringing Mother back to reality.

She opened her eyes and looked down, amazed at what she saw. Those same eyes, like big pools of ocean blue were looking up at her. Mother once again had a pang of guilt, sometimes wishing she could *not* remember. She wondered if it caused more harm than good. She leaned in and kissed Princess on the cheek, stroking her smooth, bald head—thankful for this moment, as well as the memories.

Mother softly whispered, "Go to sleep, Princess. Dream big, the world is yours for the taking."

The Song that Changed Everything
By
Lynn Hobbs

Her scissors clipped across his face as she combed and studied the white, bushy eyebrows. "Be still, you big baby." Marie shook her head at Rubin and leaned towards him.

"Handsome baby, you mean, and I've sat in this chair long enough." Rubin squirmed in an attempt to stand. Marie lunged and playfully pushed him back.

"My, aren't you something?" He laughed.

"I think I am. I can cut hair with the best of them." She grinned and poked him in the ribs. "You old fox."

Rubin pulled her to himself in one swift motion and rubbed his shaggy mop of eyebrows over her cheek.

"Ewww. That's it; those wild hairs have to go!" She cut fast and hair fell over his nose, down his neck, and on the kitchen floor. Rubin sputtered, and Marie quickly glanced at him.

"Close your mouth, I'm nearly done." A few well-placed snips and she finished. "There, good as new." She smiled at her old friend and dusted the loose hairs off of him with a hand towel.

"I can get up now?"

"Yes, you can get up now."

He stood and stretched his arms, and yawned. "My show starts in five minutes. I have a surprise for you today." Rubin turned the radio on and beamed.

Marie listened as the theme song played, "The Golden Oldies Hour." She poured them both a glass of iced tea, and Rubin set a deck of cards on the table.

"Your deal."

She shuffled cards and passed them out to play a game of Skip-Bo. "I am grateful the station manager lets you tape your program ahead of time. We can enjoy it together." She paused. "You go first."

He nodded and gathered his cards. The taped program began and his voice boomed from the radio. "And a special treat for Marie, here is a song meant just for the two of us."

She increased the volume. The smooth melody and a clear, rich voice blended as the words to, "We've Only Just Begun" sailed out into the kitchen.

"Oh, Rubin, it's Karen and Richard Carpenter! I love hearing them sing!" She reached and squeezed his hand.

"I remembered you did. I wanted to do something special. You've been working so hard on the night shift at the hospital, lately. "How much longer will you be on nights?"

"They are short-handed at the E.R. with qualified surgical nurses. I might be there another month."

"I don't see how you do it." Rubin patted her shoulder. "Let's finish this game." He yawned. *

An hour later, Rubin went to bed, and Marie dressed for work. She pulled her salt and pepper hair in a bun, applied lipstick, and grabbed her purse. A brisk walk in the night air invigorated her, and she hummed the tune she'd heard earlier. "And when the evening comes, we smile… yes…we've only just begun."

She arrived at the hospital and when the automatic doors swung open, she was immediately struck with silence.

How unusual for the E.R. to be this quiet.

She put her purse in a locker and hastened to a co-worker, Delores.

"What is this, the lull before the storm?" Marie raised an eyebrow.

"No, Marie. All patients were admitted and issued

rooms upstairs. You know, the usual shift change. Oh, wait, follow me; Fed-X left some packages in the main office." They walked down a hall when a young, attractive woman wearing nurse's scrubs approached from the opposite direction.

"I was told I had a package here."

"What's your name, and I'll look for it."

"Lena."

Delores sorted through the various size packages on the counter. "Let's see, this is for Sandy in Admitting, Trish in Maintenance, and she held one in the air. "This is for Marie-Night E.R. Nurse." She handed it to the grey-headed woman.

"And this one is for Lena; Day Shift E.R."

"That's me." The younger woman grabbed her package.

They both opened them at the same time.

"Oh, it's from Rubin, an album of the Carpenters!" Marie held it close to her chest and beamed.

"I have the same thing!" Lena glanced at the card. "And it's from my sweet Rubin." She quickly frowned at Marie. "How do you know Rubin?"

"He's my husband." Marie scowled and spoke in a voice that rose in volume, "Once a cheater, always a cheater."

Lena lifted her eyebrows and nodded. "Tell you what, let's put both of our albums in the same package and send it back to him."

"Sounds good. How about a cup of coffee?"

"I can't wait."

O My Heart!
By
Judith Victoria Douglas

O Heart! Beat On!
The world is gray
Though love is not gone,
For it is the fiber that binds
And is never loosed by sorrow.

O Heart! Break Not!
The sky is cloudy
As sadness is our lot,
But memory has its magic
Which will keep us till tomorrow.

O Heart! Bleed Less!
The wind blows ill
While love endures such emptiness,
So mend this wound that pains,
For loss has not such power.

O Heart! Ache Never!
The rain falls heavy
But the bond shall not sever,
As closer to the Veil we come,
And Time does mark our hour.

O Heart! Cry Little!
Rays of light peek through,
The façade of sadness brittle,
While knowing grows ever stronger

'Tis the Season

And hope does give a glimmer.

O Heart! Pain Cease!
The sun will shine again
And gladness give us peace,
For the faces we long to see,
And, in looking, I see a shimmer.

O Heart! Stop Now!
The sun is shining through
As our love shows us how
To recover from this life's trials
When we win and cross to meet them.

For sadness clouds the mind
And keeps us ever here,
But will be past at seeing
Loved ones in Glory, oh, so near.

From *If I Could Only Sparkle*, 2nd novella in the book *Painted Tree: Two Novellas*, as written by the main character, Tessa

On the Mend
By
Kimmie Easley

Pink streamers, pink balloons, and pink cupcakes; wall to wall decorations in every shade of pink imaginable. A billboard-size banner, draping an entire wall, scrolled with the words "It's A Girl!" (It's a good thing they clarified the gender. I would never have known!) Oh, I almost forgot. It's pink. The table, lined in pink bunting, is piled high with frilly gift bags. They overflow with pink dresses, baby bottles and other pink "necessities" donning, you guessed it, pink spiral ribbons.

I suddenly feel sick.

Pasting on a smile, I busy myself helping with refreshments and clean up duties. I try not to watch as my worthy friend opens gifts. She places each newborn outfit on her rounded belly for the perfect memory book photo. Everything about her seems to drip of sheer joy, leaving her radiant. No one deserves it more than she, especially me. Nature confirms just how undeserving I am every single day.

As the pang in my heart meets the hot tears in my eyes, I realize I am too fragile to be here. The doctor appointment this morning to discuss my infertility left me in an emotional tailspin. Here I am at another baby shower filled with bellies, babies, and toddlers at every turn. What was I thinking only hours after scheduling a hysterectomy?

Deciding to make my escape, I begin my goodbyes just as a loud woman approaches and says, "Hey, can you hold Macy while I run to the restroom? I'll only be a minute." Before I have a chance to respond, six-month-old

Macy is shoved into my arms. Her mom casually makes her way to the restroom, stopping to talk to every person in her path.

I can't help but feel the softness of her skin next to mine. Her fine hair smells of lavender. Her tiny hand grips my finger tightly. This precious little princess lay perfectly trusting, gently submissive, in my arms. She trusts me, without judgment. I want to revel in her embrace forever, to lose myself along with my broken body and spirit.

Without realizing the greatness of the moment, an unsuspecting friend-of-a-friend comes up asking the inevitable, "Awww, are you practicing for when you have your own sweet princess?"

I've run out of smiles and polite responses. Something snaps.

I blurt out, "As a matter of fact, no. I'll never have my own *sweet princess*. But thanks for asking." I leave the woman and others in earshot startled at my words, full of rage and self-pity. I find Macy's mother and shove the innocent baby in her arms and bolt for the door.

I drive a few miles before pulling off the road. Then, I allow my body to collapse.

Questions flood my thoughts. What have I done to deserve such pain? Did I do something so horrible that my punishment should be this severe? Why would God do this, leave me with a lifetime of void and heartache?

It hurts so bad, I can actually feel the ache rooted so deep in my soul. It's difficult to breathe...

Gathering myself, empty and drained, I manage to make it home only to look through the window and see James playing with Belle, a German Shepard, our only child. They're wrestling, and I can see James laughing while Belle's tail is going a hundred miles a minute. The lights from the Christmas tree are twinkling, giving the illusion of rainbow colored snow on the windowpane. My heart plummets, knowing the first thing he'll ask about is the doctor's appointment.

I want to fall into his arms and let him hold me, protect my heart, and tell me everything will be all right. I want to hear him reassure me we will have a baby, a family of our own, and life will be perfect. It's unfair to force him to lie, but I know he will—if only to soothe my aching heart.

I tell myself to suck it up. I need to be strong for James. He deserves so much more than I am able to give. He fell in love with me expecting to be a complete family. He's talked about wanting children for years, especially a girl. He wants to have his own little princess so he can paint her nursery, teach her to ride a bike, pull her first tooth, take her picture before prom and walk her down the aisle when she marries. He's already picked out the song he wants to play for their father-daughter dance. James wants to hold her when she's scared, protect her, tell her Daddy will always be there to keep her safe, and wipe away her precious princess tears.

However, today will be different.

I have to tell James that in just three short weeks I will no longer be capable of making, or carrying his child. I can never give him the one thing he wants most. How can our fate be so cruel? Me without a baby, and James burdened with a damaged wife?

After sitting in the driveway for what felt like a lifetime, I clean the black from under my swollen eyes, apply some make-up, say a little prayer, and walk through the front door.

Belle runs to meet me. I try to smile as her relief tells me I'm safely home. It feels good to have unconditional love, even if it is from a dog. James leans in for a kiss and it's clear he can read my thoughts. It's as if my day is written on my face.

He gently leads me to the sofa, pulls me in, and strokes my hair.

Here it comes, the comfort of lies.

I can hear James choke back tears. He takes in a deep

breath then says, "Don't you know I fell in love with you for your strength, for your heart, for you? I didn't fall in love with the hopeful promises of things to come. *You* are my family. We may never have a child of our own, only God knows the plans He has for our future. Just know, my life was made complete the day you stole my heart and it will stay that way as long as *you* exist."

I sit there in a heap, crying into his chest as he speaks the truth from his heart—no more lies.

"Let me love you, and only you, for as much time as God will allow. Let me wipe away your tears, keep you safe, and hold you when you're scared. I want to protect you, laugh with you, and live life with *you*."

James and I sit for hours. Belle lays her head in my lap, waiting for confirmation that I'm okay. My heart begins to stir as James' words of love override my sorrow.

Yes, today will be different. My heart is forever changed.

Today, a princess is born.

Wanted: New Home
By
Judy Walker

My master has moved to an apartment in Houston and the old Granny taking care of me wants me out of her house. I need a new home.

I come from a line of pedigreed dogs. My mother is a registered Boston terrier. Unfortunately, she got in with some street scoundrels and as a result, I don't know who my Daddy is. My Granny says she can tell me, "He ain't no teeny Boston terrier." She says I must be part Great Dane or some kind of hunting dog because I am good at hunting.

I can sniff out anything. I sniffed out a nest of baby bats in the hedge last year and frightened my Granny most to death. My master had to call out the animal control officers who came out because they were afraid we would all get rabies.

This year I cornered a possum one night, but my master wouldn't let me play with it. I do love critters. I chase them all evening. I don't know why Granny gets mad at me. It might be because of all the holes in her backyard. Just because the holes I dig are deeper than the holes the moles make in the backyard is no reason for her to get so worked up about me chasing those moles. You would think she would be happy that I could catch one.

I will tell you I have a lot of other benefits, too. I am good at killing bugs and spiders. I love playing with them and eating them.

I'm not a picky eater either. I'll eat almost anything. Just ask my Granny. She's seen me eat her purse and shoes and papers and towels and anything she likes.

Don't worry about me being like other dogs and afraid of storms and thunder and lighting and rain. I love to go out when it's raining. I will just run around in that rain and then come back in and shake off and run around the house like crazy. Granny doesn't like that either.

I've tried to tell her that when I have to tinkle, I have to go then, not later. It's up to her to decide what kind of wetness she wants on her carpet.

The only things I don't like are baths. If you even mention the word bathtub, I will run and hide under the bed. That shampoo and all that washing just creeps me out. Give me a good run in the rain, but no baths in the bathtub, please!

I love to play any kind of ball games. Soccer is my favorite. So if you have a big yard and a big heart come and adopt me. Maybe I could be your Christmas present. I'm at 903-555-5555.

The Shoe Fit the Wrong Sister
By
Lynn Hobbs

Greasy wisps of stringy hair caressed the hollow cheeks of Cinderella's gangly stepsister. At six foot four, Fay stood erect and giggled.

The sisters gathered to try on the glass slipper.

Dressed in a dusty-rose gown, stepsister, Olga, weighed in at over four hundred pounds. Her grin displayed three missing teeth; two on top and one on the bottom.

Cinderella, long-legged and attractive, had been shoved aside and was hidden behind the skirts of her ugly stepsisters.

All eyes were on the Prince. He approached in a carriage pulled by a pair of horses. Coughing, he placed the back of a hand against his mouth. "Do three sisters live here, or is it four?"

His question hung in the air, and no one answered.

A quick leap and he disembarked. He scanned the growing crowd of women as his footman carried a glass slipper upon a burgundy pillow. Heavy blends of perfume assaulted his nostrils. He applied pressure with his pinky finger above the corner of his mouth and prevented a sneeze.

Olga sauntered towards the Prince and spicy aroma followed. She held her petticoats with one hand and tried to ease her foot into the slipper. After several futile attempts, she grimaced, and backed away.

He spotted Cinderella, in her brown homespun. She met his gaze, and they shared a tentative smile. She looked away, and he kept staring at her. Homespun or not, her presence was noticed. She carried herself as ladylike as a noblewoman. She lifted her eyes and they shared another warmer smile. Abruptly, Fay, the tall stepsister, shoved Cinderella against the wall of the building behind her.

"Let me try." She cackled, and demanded of the Prince. Quite against the insistence of his pounding heart, he bowed politely. "Madam."

Fay put her foot inside the slipper, and it fit perfectly.

Wide-eyed, the Prince turned pale as the tall sister and the entire crowd gasped out loud together.

"No, oh no, I haven't had my turn." Cinderella whimpered and rushed to the Prince.

"Too late." The tall sister yelled, and people milling around took up the chant, and the noise grew in volume. "Too late. Too late."

Horses opened their mouths and whinnied. Their handlers quickly and expertly calmed them with firm commands.

Cinderella grasped the slipper, noticed the glare of her stepsister, and tried it on.

No, the glass slipper didn't fit Cinderella's foot.

A low hush fell over the crowd as she returned the slipper back to the Prince. The moment was suddenly interrupted by another woman.

"I'm a stepsister, let me try too." A woman pranced about, flinging her green skirts to and fro.

A chorus of "So am I. I'm also a stepsister." could be heard from women scattered throughout the crowd.

"Enough. All of you back off," the Prince ordered.

He looked up at the stepsister who towered above him and narrowed his eyes at her. "Your foot fit the slipper. You will be my Princess; however, I do not remember dancing with anyone as tall as you."

Cinderella stepped forward. "It was I who was your dancing partner. My feet are swollen today, and I cannot wear the slipper." She hung her head in obvious sorrow.

"I have to stand on my word. I had said whose foot fits the slipper will be my Princess. So be it."

He motioned for the taller girl, and she hurried to stand by his side. "I will display you as an example of keeping my word."

He quickly turned to Cinderella, grabbed her rough hands and examined her calluses. "Your hard work has paid off, Cinderella. I will give all of my horses to you as a new business venture."

He pivoted to the crowd. "Hear ye, hear ye. Be it known, as of this hour Cinderella is the owner of the magnificent roadsters."

Cinderella clapped her hands together and jumped up and down, squealing with laughter.

A loud cheer sailed forth, and he reached to hold the hand of his potential Princess. He helped her into the carriage, and they drove off amid happy shouts and applause.

Princess Envy
By
Kimmie Easley

Princess grew stronger by the day. Mother couldn't help but watch her daughter with a good dose of healthy envy. It was rare to see someone so young embrace their trials, especially when they were worn on the outside for the whole world to see. As Princess seemed to become more powerful and take on the responsibility God had bestowed upon her, Mother struggled with her own feelings. She lay in bed at night almost ashamed. She did not understand why she felt so weak, and in the dark, unable to move forward like Princess. After all she was older, meant to be the example to her young, impressionable daughter. Instead she was full of guilt, and no matter how hard she tried, she couldn't shake it. It began to dig at her very being. It crushed her to know she would never be able to fix Princess's problem. This thought devastated her heart.

Mother sat on the park bench, feeling the chill in the air as it announced autumn was soon on the way out. She tried to lose her thoughts in the pages of someone else's story, but her focus continued to wander back to the playground. Princess was playing with a small group of children. It always amazed Mother how quickly children befriended one another. Her eyes fixed on Princess and her smile. She was dressed for fall, wearing a cozy sweater paired with her favorite scarf. Her boots left muddy tracks along the path from the recent rain. As she ran, the pompom on her beanie cap bounced up and down. Mother looked around and noticed she was dressed much like the other children. Princess giggled and let out peals of laughter as she jumped off of a swing landing in the dirt.

The next thing to happen brought Mother to her feet. Princess reached up and pulled off her cap. Mother could tell she wasn't thinking about what she was doing, she was simply rubbing her head. Mother's eyes darted to the other children, ready to run to Princess's side to swoop her up and out of harm's way. The little boys and girls looked at her, then at each other. Mother knew there were words spoken because mouths were moving. Finally, Princess nodded and lowered her head.

"Oh no!" Mother said out loud.

To her astonishment, the little girl touched the top of Princess's head as they both smiled. The little boy tapped her arm and took off running. Immediately, Princess was on his tail ready to tag.

Mother realized she had been holding her breath since the moment her feet hit the ground. She took a deep breath and steadied herself against a tree.

Mother instantly knew the only problem Princess had at the moment was the need to make it to base before being caught. Mother decided the only fixing that needed to be done was to her very own heart.

'Tis the Season

Biographies

Elizabeth Baker

Elizabeth Baker, Ph.D. is the author, speaker, and avid gardener. A widow since her mid-30's, she proudly claims four, fantastic children, fifteen remarkable grandchildren, and six amazing great-grands. Yet, she identifies her greatest joy as helping others apply biblical principles to real-life situations.

Visit her website to read her personal testimony, find out about available books, or sign up to have weekly devotions delivered to your inbox. Contact Elizabeth directly at ebaker@ElizabethBakerBooks.com

Webisite: www.elizabethbakerbooks.com
FaceBook: facebook.com/grannywritesbooks
Twitter: @granny_writes
Email: ebaker@elizabethbakerbooks.com

Jeannie Faulkner Barber

Jeannie Faulkner Barber was born and raised in Marshall, Texas. There are two passions in her life: writing and drag racing. She even met her husband, Monte, at the drag strip and can boast of winning the most trophies and cash at the pulse-pounding sport. Joan Hallmark, with KLTV 7 in Tyler, Texas, did a dual interview with her on *Proud of East Texas* regarding these two polar-opposite interests.

Jeannie and Monte live in Kilgore, Texas and have three grown sons and nine beautiful grandchildren. She works for the Overton-New London Chamber of Commerce as Office Manager and Executive Vice President, is a member of the board for East Texas Writers Association (ETWA), member of North East Texas Writers Organization (NETWO), and a three-time winner of NaNoWriMo.

Taste of Fire, is a dynamic mystery about a female firefighter, has been number one on Goodreads.com as Best Modern Mystery, Crime Fiction for over a year. With a sequel in the works. Her enthralling fantasy, *Destiny Never Sleeps* series was co-authored with Bernadette Thompson Martin of South Carolina. Book one is *Quest of the Two Queens.* Another novel by Jeannie is *Scent of Double Deception,* a contemporary suspense. All her works are available on *Amazon* and *Barnes & Noble.*

The Pen Temptress: www.jeanniefaulknerbarber.blogspot.com
Website: http://www.jeanniebarber.com
 http://www.destinyneversleeps.com.
Facebook Jeannie Faulkner Barber
Twitter @dragracers22
Email: dragracer2@yahoo.com

Jeannie is always available for personal appearances or guest speaker requests.

Vivra P. Beene

Vivra is an award-winning writer, poet, and artist. Welsh by birth, English by raising, and Texan by marriage, Vivra has taken root in the East Texas Piney Woods with her husband and three dachshunds. She has had work published in various newspapers and magazines (including Alfred Hitchcock's Mystery Magazine) and she has received awards from the Society of Children's Book Writers and Illustrators, Writer's Digest, the Gregg County and Rusk County Poetry Societies, and from the East Texas Writer's Association.

Among Vivra's non-writing interests are painting, sketching, and creating greeting cards; reading; listening to (good) music; fishing and bowling—and sometimes, when the mood hits, knitting.

Vivra likes to write short stories involving "Paranormal Punishments for the Perpetrators of the Perceived Perfect Crime" and is currently working on a young adult novel with a paranormal theme set in her home country, England.

Blog: vivratalks.wordpress.com
Facebook Vivra Patricia Beene
Email: vivrabeene@suddenlink.net

Evelyn M. Byrne

Evelyn M. Byrne, Best Selling Author of the Daughter of Prophecy Series. Born in Dublin, Ireland, Evelyn grew up in Chicago, Illinois. Lived in Tucson, Arizona, for eight years and currently resides in East Texas with her husband, Kevin and Old English Sheepdogs, Bridie and Maggie. She loves reading paranormal romances and with her extensive travels back to Ireland, her writing instinctively gravitated toward Irish mythology.

"Other writers portray the Tuatha Dé Danann either as tricksters or deadly fae (fairies). I decided to bring them into the same light as some of my favorite authors did with vampires and weres. So now, we have vamps, weres, and fae all living in our neighborhoods and don't even know it," says Ms. Byrne.

She served as president of the East Texas Writers Association from 2007 through 2011 and is currently serving as treasurer. She is also a member of the East Texas Writers Guild, North East Writers' Organization, Romance Writers of America, Fantasy, Futuristic and Paranormal, and the Kiss of Death. You can find her books at *Amazon, Barnes & Noble,* and *White Bird Publications.*

Website: http://www.evelynmbyrne.com
Facebook: facebook.com/evelynmbyrne
Author Page: http://goo.gl/Hq5B9
Twitter: http://twitter.com/EvelynMByrne
Blog: http://evelynmbyrne.blogspot.com/
Email: evelynmbyrne@gmail.com
White Bird Publications: http://www.whitebirdpublications.com

Brinda Carey

Brinda Carey earned a Bachelor of Science degree in Criminal Justice from UTT and is a retired probation officer from Smith County. Her book, *Don't Cry, Daddy's Here*, shares her personal story of survival and recovery from a childhood of incest. Brinda is a member of the RAINN Speakers Bureau and accepts speaking engagements to inform the public about the ongoing problem of child abuse and to offer hope for those in recovery. She also speaks at writers' conferences and workshops on the craft of writing. Each month, she teaches life-booking and writing skills to the young women of Saving Grace.

A native Texan, Brinda now resides in Northwest Arkansas where her husband of thirty years is currently employed. Their children and thirteen grandchildren bring much joy into their lives, as does their Springer spaniel, Maggie Mae. Favorite past-times include reading, traveling, dining, and theater.

Website: www.brindacarey.com
Facebook: https://www.facebook.com/brinda.carey.author?fref=ts
        https://www.facebook.com/DONTCRYDADDYSHERE
Twitter: https://twitter.com/brindacarey
Blog: www.brindacarey.com
Email: brinda.carey1@gmail.com

Judith Victoria Douglas

Judith Victoria Douglas is a pseudonym for Judith Lee. Judith was born in Philadelphia, but has lived in Texas since an infant. Now retired, Judith has resided in East Texas for over twelve years on a few quiet acres with her German Shepherd, Belle. She completed a Master's of Science in Counseling Psychology, and a Bachelor's in Psychology and is a lifetime member of Psi Chi, National Honor Society for Psychology. She had previous experience with the Department of the Army as a civilian in several capacities and with Potter County Adult Probation before teaching upper level University psychology classes at the formerly named University of Central Texas (now Central Texas A & M University) while working full time. Her longest tenure was as a case manager for public assistance programs in Central and East Texas with her latest position as a quality assurance monitor of those programs. She's also worked with at-risk youth and women recovering from substance abuse problems. Judith also owned and trained horses, and gave riding lessons for a number of years, competing and coaching students in a variety of equestrian events, her passion being *Dressage*. She's also modeled, been part of different choir organizations, and studied the piano, organ and violin

Website: http://www.judithvictoriadouglas.com
Facebook: http://www.facebook.com/authorjudithvictoriadouglas
Twitter: http://www.twitter.com/booksbyjvd
LinkedIn: http://www.linkedin.com/in/jvdouglas1
Blogs: https://www.booksbyjudithvictoriadouglas.wordpress.com
  https://www.jvdbooks.tumblr.com
  https://www.blogspot.com/judithvictoriadoulgas
  https://www.booksbyjvd.wordpress.com
Email: books@judithvictoriadouglas.com

Kimmie Easley

Kimmie Easley grew up traveling the country, rarely settling in one place for much longer than a minute. She and her husband Daniel, an East Texas native, along with their two daughters have now made Northeast Texas their home. The Easley family's favorite past time is traveling to nearby small towns and learning about southern traditions and culture, frequenting festivals, museums, bookstores and libraries. Kimmie also spends her time home-schooling, writing and reading (her first love).

Kimmie is currently working on her first novel. She is a 2012 NaNoWriMo (National Novel Writing Month) winner and is currently serving as secretary to the East Texas Writers Association.

Kimmie started writing her first masterpiece at ten years old, although she's known to be a little bias. Being no stranger to heartache, she allows her unconventional childhood to serve as fuel for her writing style. Kimmie writes realistic fiction as well as short stories in various genres. Her Princess collection is inspired by her daughter and is written in hopes of bringing to light the heart of a family struggling with Alopecia Areata. Kimmie and her family are great advocates within the AA community.

Website: KimmieEasley.com
Facebook: facebook.com/kimmie.easley
Twitter: twitter.com/KimmieAnnWrites
Blog: http://anneasley.blogspot.com/
Email: kanneasley@aol.com

Janice Ernest

Janice Ernest is an up-and-coming author who lives in East Texas with her mom and two dogs, Patsy and Pearl. She has owned, operated, and published *WhileUWait* Magazine and her work has been seen in newspapers, magazines, and, in its latest debut, on Kindle in the form of a fun series of books entitled, *Brocksport, The Maynard Junebug Series*, and *Brocksport, Back Again*. Her belief is that writing is an adventure in learning and she seeks daily to enlarge her knowledge base and bring better manuscripts to the table with each completed project.

Website: www.janiceernest.com
Twitter: https://twitter.com/JaniceErnest
Email: janiceernest1@gmail.com

Ann Everett

Ann Everett is a Texas girl from her big-bar-hair down to her bare toes. For many years she did stand-up comedy for businesses, corporations, and non-profit organizations.

Creator of the White Trash Facelift, halter tops, and beer bling bracelets, Ann embraces her small town upbringing and thinks Texans are the funniest people on earth.

She's an award winning author and active member of Northeast Texas Writers' Organization.

When Ann's not writing, she spends her days listening in on people's conversations at the local Wal-Mart, beauty shop, grocery store, and numerous other gathering spots. She draws from that research to pen her novels full of southern sass and Texas twang. Books are available on *Amazon* and *Barnes & Noble*.

Website: www.anneverett.com
Facebook: https://www.facebook.com/TalkinTwang?fref=ts
Twitter: twitter.com/TalkinTwang
Blog: www.anneverett.com/Talkin'Twang
Amazon: Shttp://goo.gl/9YgBM
Barnes & Noble: http://www.barnesandnoble.com/c/ann-everett
Email: ann.everett@rocketmail.com

Lynn Hobbs

Lynn Hobbs is a member of GFWC-Texas Federation of Women's Clubs–Marshall Chapter, American Christian Fiction Writers, Pens: Crosswords Christian Writers, East Texas Christian Writers, North East Texas Writers Organization, past treasurer (2011-2012) of East Texas Writers Association, and a Lifetime member of World Wide Who's Who.

Retired from the Texas public school system—Lynn is available for speaking engagements.

World Wide Who's Who awarded Lynn Hobbs Professional of the Year 2012-2013 in Authorship. The Author Show.com named Lynn as a finalist in their nationwide contest; "Fifty Great Authors You Should Be Reading in 2012.

Author of a powerful faith and family saga, the Running Forward Series.

Book one—*Sin, Secrets, and Salvation.* A Christian wife, Susan Penleigh is unequally yoked to a non-Christian husband. Follow her victorious journey through a shaky marriage. Scripture, prayer, and intrigue round out this inspiring novel.

Book two—*River Town.* Susan relocates to Texas during the worst drought in history with terrifying wildfires, and a new job at a high school. Readers will understand a Christian viewpoint by Susan's actions. Books are available on *Amazon* and *Barnes & Noble.*

Website: http://www.lynnhobbsauthor.com/
Facebook author page: http://goo.gl/7znDp
Facebook: https://www.facebook.com/lynn.hobbs.3367?ref=tn_tnmn
Twitter: https://twitter.com/LynnHobbsAuthor
LinkedIn: http://goo.gl/T8r4V
Amazon: http://www.amazon.com/-/e/B006X0YX0E
Barnes & Noble: http://www.barnesandnoble.com/c/lynn-hobbs
Email: LynnHobbs.Author@gmail.com

Gay Ingram

Gay Ingram began her writing career as a result of a passionate interest in herbs. She published a bi-monthly newsletter for five years along with several informational booklets and soft cover books about herbs. A creative writing course offered by Tyler Junior College launched Ms. Ingram into fiction writing. Her first novel, 'Til Death Do Us Part, was released in 2001 followed by a history of her hometown of Big Sandy, Texas, Tracks On The Sand. Her second novel, Troubled Times, came out in 2005 and Twist of Fate, her most recent novel became available in 2010. In her long writing career, Gay Ingram has enjoyed the rewards of sharing about courageous ordinary people experiencing extraordinary circumstances. Books are available on *Amazon, Barnes & Noble* and *White Bird Publications*.

Website: http://www.gayingram.webs.com
       http://www.pineywoodsbooks.webs.com
Facebook: https://www.facebook.com/gay.ingram?fref=ts
Twitter: https://twitter.com/IngramGay
Blog: http://www.gayingram.blogspot.com/
Amazon: https://www.amazon.com/author/gayingram
Barnes & Noble: http://goo.gl/lClFH
Email: gaymingram@gmail.com

Simon Lang

Simon Lang/Darlene Artell Hartman," began writing professionally in the early 1950's for The Hour of St. Francis, then the largest private film studio west of the Mississippi. Her PSA's during the Desegregation Crisis were written up in Newsweek Magazine; and her novice film, "Victory," won the Catholic Academy for Communication Arts Professionals "Gabriel" Award, and introduced a young Jack Nicholson. She went on to write five scripts for the original Star Trek, and was on staff, as she says, "for about 20 minutes," until ill health sidelined her television
writing career. She has three more novels on the way, as well as several more books in the Einai Series.

Simon's books are available on *Amazon, Barnes & Noble* and *White Bird Publications.*

Website: http://www.authorsimonlang.com
Facebook: https://www.facebook.com/simon.lang.319?fref=ts
Twitter: https://twitter.com/AuthorSimonLang
Blog:
Amazon: http://goo.gl/7BVUS
Barnes & Noble: http://www.barnesandnoble.com/c/simon-lang
Email: simonlang.lang3@gmail.com

Jean Lauzier

Jean Lauzier was born and raised in Arkansas. She now lives in Longview with her husband and three children. When not writing, you can find Jean talking to her bonsai plants, trying to train the cat or procrastinating on the computer.

She is a member of the East Texas Writers' Association and has now taken the title of President. Jean is a member of North East Texas Writers Organization and East Texas Christian Writers.

Her short stories have been published by Mysterical-e, Golden Visions, Crimson Dagger, Mouthful of Bullets and numerous other places along with winning several contests. In addition, Jean writes a weekly column about writing for Long Ridge Writer's Group.

Her books are available on *Amazon, Barnes & Noble* and *White Bird Publications.*

Blog: http://www.jeanlauzier.com.
FaceBook: https://www.facebook.com/jeanlauzier2319
Twitter: https://twitter.com/#!/jeanlauzier
Email: jeanlauzier@gmail.com
Amazon: http://goo.gl/Ikm2C
Barnes & Noble: http://goo.gl/3wJjQ

C. R. Myers

    C. R. Myers, a native Texan, received her MA from the University of Texas at Tyler. As a teacher and professional speaker, she designed and implemented her own creative writing course as well as writing college sketches. Today, Ms. Myers works full-time as a free-lance journalist and novelist.

    C. R. Myers writes mystery and suspense—cozy to edgy and enjoys having a well-developed plot with lots of surprises.

    Ms. Myers writes children's books. As a child she was an incessant reader. As a teacher and mother, she witnessed the joy children experience reading stories for themselves, especially those incorporating rhythm and rhyme. In the process of creating a new book, she envisions the pleasure the child will receive when hearing or reading the story. Ms. Myers prefers a story to have some teaching value while still being entertaining.

    Growing up, C. R. Myers developed a fondness for serial stories. She looked forward to the delivery of the weekly paper with the latest chapter in an ongoing novel. Early in her writing career she wrote serial novels for several papers and magazines in her area as well as online. She is excited to participate in the Kindle venture of serial fiction.

Website: http://www.crmyers.com
Facebook: https://www.facebook.com/cathyrmyers?fref=ts
Twitter: https://twitter.com/crmyers
Blog: http://www.crmyers.blogspot.com
Email: crmyers11@gmail.com
Amazon: http://goo.gl/dql6Q
Barnes & Noble: http://www.barnesandnoble.com/c/c.-r.-myers

Kimberli O'Brien

Kimberli O'Brien was born and raised in a small East Texas town where she now lives with her husband and their two children. She is a full time wife and mother who enjoys writing fiction and poetry and editing in her spare time. She loves spending time with her family outdoors. Kimberli also helps manage the children's ministry at her church and teaches the preschool class.

Blog: Kimberliobrien.blogspot.com
Email: kimberliobrien@gmail.com

Kassy Paris

Kassy Paris, is half of the writing team known as Kasandra Elaine, a partnership made up of two best friends, Kassy Paris and Elaine Bonner, who met as sophomores in high school.

When Kassy and Elaine announced to their families their intention to write and become published, they received skepticism and laughter. Yet, they persevered and achieved their goals. To date, the friends have been published four times and continue to write. Currently, Kassy and Elaine are working on the first book in a cozy mystery series.

In pursuit of a solo publishing career, Kassy is in the revision process for books one and two of a romantic suspense series and is writing book three.

Kassy is also a freelance editor. Besides acting as the final editor for all four of Kasandra Elaine's published books, Kassy has edited published books for Peggy Blann Phifer, Evelyn M. Byrne, and Karen Latham.

Kassy spent 20 years as an elementary school teacher for Marshall ISD in Marshall, Texas. Among her other interests are traveling, reading, collecting minerals, and quilting. As a quilter, she designs and creates small wall hangings she calls Greeting Card Quilts.

Website: http://www.kasandraelainebooks.com/
Facebook: https://www.facebook.com/kassy.paris.3?ref=ts&fref=ts
Email: kmparis@hotmail.com
Amazon: http://goo.gl/y8Xlg
Barnes & Noble: http://goo.gl/Utn8H

Larence Shaddox

Larence Shaddox tells a funny sorry about himself. As a kid he hated books, At least until he was fourteen. Then he discovered the Hardy Boys series, John Carter of Mars series, followed by the abundant worlds of science fiction and fantasy.

He has managed to do a lot of traveling. Spending time in several countries around the world on active duty in the military and afterwards traveled to a large portion of the United States. All the while he was an avid reader. Inspire by his English 101 instructor, he started writing stories for his own entertainment and has for years. Recently he started working to get his first novel published. He has several articles and short stories published and has received several awards for short pieces. He is currently serving as the vice president of the East Texas Writers Association where he has been learning to improve his skills as a writer.

He gets his inspirations from the early writers of science fiction and fantasy. With some of his stories he manages to put in bits of adventures from his own life as many writers do.

Now-a-days, he spends his free time reclusive in the piney woods of East Texas working on his stories with his favorite companion, a dachshund named Sweets.

Facebook: https://www.facebook.com/larence.shaddox?fref=ts
Twitter: https://twitter.com/LarenceShaddox
Email:larenceshaddox@gmail.com

Judy Walker

Judy Walker is a retired school librarian residing in White Oak, Texas. She still works part-time at H&R Block, but enjoys her other activities such as spending time with her two grandchildren after school, volunteering for Meals on Wheels, and assistant librarian at the church and volunteer at her grandchildren's school library. She's been published in the School Library Journal and Theatre of the Mind.

Facebook: https://www.facebook.com/judy.walker.750983?fref=ts
LinkedIn: http://goo.gl/Amedy
Email: JWalker658@sbcglobal.net

Denny Youngblood

A native Texan, Denny Youngblood currently resides in Longview, Texas with his beautiful wife Alice. He earned his Eagle Scout award at age 16 and later went on to serve his country in the U.S. Air Force. His earned Ph.D. in Psychology has helped him pen several novels, short stories, and non-fiction works. In his spare time, he enjoys drawing and painting Western art, and is an accomplished musician. He also serves as a deacon at his church. His wife, children, and grandchildren make his life complete.

Facebook: https://www.facebook.com/denny.youngblood?fref=ts
Amazon Author Page: http://goo.gl/fmrtW
Blog: http://dennyyoungblood.blogspot.com/
Email: denny.youngblood@yahoo.com

CPSIA information can be obtained at www.ICGtesting.com
Printed in the USA
LVOW120441250613

339884LV00001B/1/P